Books by GEOFFREY HOUSEHOLD

Novels

THE THIRD HOUR

ROGUE MALE

ARABESQUE

THE HIGH PLACE

A ROUGH SHOOT

A TIME TO KILL

FELLOW PASSENGER

WATCHER IN THE SHADOWS

THING TO LOVE

OLURA

THE COURTESY OF DEATH

DANCE OF THE DWARFS

Autobiography

AGAINST THE WIND

Short Stories

THE SALVATION OF PISCO GABAR

TALES OF ADVENTURERS

THE BRIDES OF SOLOMON

SABRES ON THE SAND

For Children

THE EXPLOITS OF XENOPHON

THE SPANISH CAVE

PRISONER OF THE INDIES

DANCE
OF THE
DWARFS

DANCE
OF THE
DWARFS

by GEOFFREY HOUSEHOLD

An Atlantic Monthly Press Book

LITTLE, BROWN AND COMPANY · BOSTON · TORONTO

Akron

ATLANTIC–LITTLE, BROWN BOOKS
ARE PUBLISHED BY
LITTLE, BROWN AND COMPANY
IN ASSOCIATION WITH
THE ATLANTIC MONTHLY PRESS

Published simultaneously in Canada
by Little, Brown & Company (Canada) Limited

PRINTED IN THE UNITED STATES OF AMERICA

DANCE
OF THE
DWARFS

Preface

IT WILL be remembered that the death of Dr. Owen
Dawnay was attributed to partisans of the Colombian
National Liberation Army. The evidence of his only
neighbors, a few families of squatters and masterless
cattlemen, appeared conclusive. They had been terror-
ized into supplying cattle to guerrilla headquarters in
the foothills of the Cordillera. Two of them had been
brutally murdered. The headman of their village had
disappeared. Dawnay himself was known to have been
threatened.

That a guerrilla detachment did indeed visit Dawnay's experimental station about the time of his death is
certain. His arms, his official journal and all his papers
were stolen. The main gate had been forced, and the
tracks of a jeep were plainly to be seen in the compound. The Colombian Government and the Ministry of
Overseas Development had every reason to suppose that
he had been executed for refusing to collaborate with
the revolutionaries.

Dawnay's choice of an agricultural station in that remote corner where the great grasslands, or llanos, at
last disappear under tropical forest, largely untraveled,
was scientifically sound, but may have owed still more
to his personal tastes. Born and bred in the south of
Argentina, he was a superb horseman and an excellent
shot with gun or rifle. Undoubtedly he enjoyed the
primitive conditions of his life and the still more primitive society of llaneros in which he found himself.

His supreme self-confidence often inclined him to be
impatient with what he considered unnecessary anxiety. His silence therefore aroused little concern, especially since the pilot of the Government Canoe which
had called at Santa Eulalia on May 2, 1966, reported
that he was in the best of health and spirits. Another
month was allowed to go by before a light aircraft was
dispatched to his station with mail, supplies and two
administrators of the Intendencia.

His house was a scene of utter desolation. Fungi were
growing in the rooms and wasps building under the
eaves. Shut in a larger inner room were the carcasses of
two horses which had died from starvation and lack of
water. Dawnay's two servants had vanished, perhaps
liquidated as the only witnesses to the murder, perhaps
panic-stricken.

The compound, which had been intensively cultivated, was turned into rank jungle by the rains. Hidden
by the vegetation were the skeletons of Dr. Dawnay and
a young female. Birds and insects had picked them

[4]

clean. Poinsettia and a twisted citrus sapling were growing through the bones. Both appeared to have been shot. The position of the bodies suggested that the executioners, with macabre sentimentality, had permitted the pair to die in each other's arms.

Though Dawnay was only thirty-three, his great promise in his own field of research was internationally recognized. As a man, he was known and loved by a host of Latin American friends in Colombia and Argentina. His death therefore aroused a storm of indignation against Cuban-financed revolutionaries. This bitterly hostile publicity may have accounted for the mysterious reappearance of his papers.

In November 1966 a black, insect-proof, metal box bearing Dawnay's initials was delivered to the publishers of his fascinating monograph *Fodder Plants of the New World.* It contained the missing journal as well as this unexpected personal diary, which was in his handwriting and undoubtedly genuine.

The motive of the anonymous senders may be inferred. Unable to clear themselves of the brutal murder of a man whom in fact they seem to have admired, they realized that the diary supplied a complete answer to the accusation against them. It seems probable that, after examining his correspondence, they found no other trustworthy address — such as that of a firm of solicitors or a learned body — and therefore chose to return the box to Dawnay's publishers, rejecting the Agricultural Mission itself as insufficiently neutral.

[5]

The unfinished entry of May 18, which must have remained on his desk until the partisans recovered it, was discolored and spotted by damp, but still decipherable. A note in Spanish had been added: *We found no weapon by the bodies. It is to be supposed that he rushed to the door to confirm that his anxiety was needless, and saw what was behind her. There was no time to go back for steel or gun, so he went on bare-handed; and whether she was alive or dead when he took her in his arms we do not know.*

The Diary of Dr. Owen Dawnay

[*March 9, Wednesday*]

I HAVE recently noticed a tendency to talk to myself. One-sided conversation is humiliating and settles nothing. It is exclamatory. It points at things which are worth remembering, but does not commit them to memory. That is my reason for starting a diary. I want to marshal the facts of my relationship to my environment and compel myself to think about them.

I also need to be able to turn back time and feel what sort of person I was two or three months before. In that way I shall spot any inclination to become a work hermit or to exaggerate this background sense of insecurity — well, not exactly of insecurity but of something unfinished — which I am unable to analyze. I suppose all missionaries suffer from the same questioning of the self.

It amuses Santa Eulalia when I describe myself as a missionary. They have nicknamed me El Misionero.

But a field agronomist of the British Tropical Agricultural Mission is surely a missionary. My bishop
and archdeacon sit in Bogotá, their chapel being an air-
conditioned office and their altar a laboratory. I, since I
am a fair horseman and bilingual in Spanish and English, was sent abroad to preach the gospel — or rather
practice it — between the rivers Guaviare and Vichada.

I chose the site myself. The others didn't know
enough to argue. I thought at first that my chief objec-
tive should be testing the right varieties of cereals. I
now see that the primeval problem of agriculture —
when to plant — is far more important. The dry season
normally begins at the end of December. This year we
have had no rain at all since December 3. But provided
God is a good man, as they say, one can grow prac-
tically anything in half the time it takes anywhere else.
This is the no man's land between savannah and forest:
the last, forgotten, blind alley of grass. To the west and
south it is bounded by darkness. To the north the llanos
spread out towards Venezuela, empty under the blazing
sun.

A perfect experimental station. It was never my intention nor that of the Mission that I should be alone on
it; but in practice I found that assistants only increased
my responsibilities. I settled in four months ago accompanied by a most friendly Colombian and a young
Minnesota Swede from the Peace Corps. I am not sure
what qualities he was supposed to have, but it was only
too clear that training by a war corps would have been

more to the point. Estrellera threw him into the creek. He missed deliberately when shooting for the pot. Then he broke out in boils and was absurdly horrified when I wanted him to try Joaquín's efficacious herbal remedies. I admit that Joaquín produces his pastes by chewing rather than pestle and mortar, but saliva is a disinfectant.

So I had him flown out. My other young friend went along to look after him, promising a swift return. I shall not see him again, which is a pity, for he was a qualified botanist and I am not. But he preferred the problems of classification and the pleasure of dictating his results to an obliging secretary after hours. The girl either wore no bra at all or had some compensating device of elastic hitherto unknown to me. I regret that I was always too busy for detailed investigation. When I return to Bogotá, I shall make a point of satisfying my curiosity.

[*March 10, Thursday*]

I don't seem to have got very far yesterday evening. I rode straight at my blank page and then began to passage sideways like Tesoro when he mistakes a barred shadow for a snake. I started off to analyze the sense of the unfinished, dabbled in the bras of Bogotá and then strolled out to the corral to see the horses. Because I wanted company or because I have recently become uneasy about them?

[9]

Certainly Tesoro and Estrellera were very glad to see me. They always are. The horse's capacity for affection never fails to surprise me. A rather stupid, nervous creature, full of love. Like some primitive, laborious Roman slave taking to Christianity when it first appeared.

During the last ten days or so they have had fits of restlessness at night; they are near enough — physically and telepathically — to be able to communicate it. They need not worry. The adobe walls of the corral are still fairly perpendicular, and jaguar on the open llano is most unlikely. Still, one must not assume that two trusted friends are liars.

Leaving out mere nuisances, such as insects and occasional slight fevers, there is less here to be afraid of than in London. On the edge of the forest one could conceivably be in trouble with a very rash or very hungry jaguar, but the risk is less than that of being charged by a drunken driver whom unfortunately one is not allowed to shoot. You could be caught on foot by wild cattle, but you take the same care not to be as you take crossing Oxford Street in the rush hour. You could be bitten by a snake, but that is hardly more likely than electrocuting yourself among the infinite dangers of a modern flat, a paralysis for which there is no serum. I have two phials. Alternatively, I could do worse than put my trust in Joaquín whose concoction of dried venom sacs and gallbladders is reinforced by his confident bedside manner. No, the greatest danger is man just as anywhere else. A band of poor, half-starved devils of the National Liberation Army occupies the wild foothills of the Cordillera, some four days hard riding to the northwest. These guerrilleros must know of my existance, and so I presume they think me harmless. As for my other neighbors, the llaneros of Santa Eulalia, we are on most cordial terms drunk or sober.

Thus physical danger may be ruled out in my search for an influence to fill what I call the blank spot. A too imaginative curiosity due to loneliness? Well, I am not all that lonely and I am neither superstitious nor skeptical. If duendes exist, as Joaquín insists they do, I am eager to meet a specimen illusion, for one cannot begin to explain until one has experienced. I play with the speculation that, just as the collective hysteria of a crowd can persuade it to see angels or flying saucers, so the rampant, hourly visible growth of the forest might produce a communal spirit, a vegetable emanation which could be detected by animal senses. Harness the green power and what green fingers it could give to an agronomist! Duende is a more comprehensive name than our ghost or elemental.

Then the house itself? But I enjoy its solidity in so much emptiness. It is a deserted estancia dating from colonial days, built square and defensible like a legionary fort. I find in it the peace of some forgotten patio where others walked and were content. On the south side are a few still-habitable, dilapidated rooms of the boss's house in which I camp. On the north are the peons' quarters: a row of ruinous shacks hung with the black combs of wasps' nests where the shade of wall and roof has encouraged a rank growth of weak lianas. These two sides of the square are joined by adobe walls a couple of hundred yards long, so that a space of some two and a half acres is enclosed. This was originally intended to provide food for the small community and is irrigated by tiled channels, barred where they pass under the walls, drawing water from the marshes to the north.

The marshes? Well, all marshes are mysterious in the half-light of dawn or dusk when the wildfowl chuckle and the canes and rushes, disturbed at their roots by some eel or amphibian, seem to swing away from the passage of the invisible. The creek which takes the overflow passes close to the estancia and runs south to an unknown confluence with the Guaviare. Two miles beyond the creek is the blue wall of the forest which I find neither friendly nor unfriendly. It is simply an overpowering fact of the planet: a barrier like the sea with its own specialized life and methods of travel.

It seems to be either forest or creek which upsets the horses. Last week I walked as far as the water's edge to see if I could spot puma on the llano or an anaconda watching the shallows where peccary or tapir might be drinking — though I believe they never come so far from the trees. I was only aware of star-lit silence, emphasized by the whine of the mosquitoes. This silence

[12]

itself sometimes produces a feeling of awe, a prickling of the scalp. So I cannot definitely say that I was uneasy. I did perhaps feel that I was observed. Hostile? No. For the moment a neutral observer like myself.

[*March 12, Saturday*]

I have come to the conclusion that the blank spot is due neither to me nor to this essentially welcoming country which waits to be inhabited. The thing which is unfinished is in the collective mind of my companions. So I will try to dissect them as individuals and see if description forces me into clear thinking.

Our isolation is sufficiently complete to eliminate all outside influences. Now that a man can take a package tour to Antarctica and cross the Sahara in his own car, the immense plains of Colombia and Venezuela and the tropical forest which forms their southern boundary must be the last expanse of world to be left as it was. In the llanos there is nothing unknown or unexplored; they are merely empty and their life has hardly changed in four hundred years. The forest, too, is known in the sense that all navigable rivers are navigated and that here and there some prospector, rubber collector or deliberate explorer has crossed by land from one river to another; but what he could see on low ground was limited to a hundred yards on either side, and on high ground to the world of the treetops. One assumes that the fauna, the flora and the floor of leaf

[13]

mold are always the same. It is, I think, a very large assumption. I have plenty of evidence pointing to rapid differentiation of species. But that is for my journal, not this diary.

I have found the Intendencia, which administers this territory, vaguely benevolent, but it does not greatly affect our lives. There are regular air services to Puerto Ayacucho and to San José del Guaviare; but one is five hundred miles away and the other a mere clump of huts to be reached eventually by canoe if a canoe is available. There is also the occasional plane to Colombia's Amazonas province. It will come down on the Guaviare at Santa Eulalia if I can advise the Mission that I need it.

A big "if." When I decided on my station, the Government — after trying its best to convince me that it was too isolated for what they called a cultured European — told me that at least I should have excellent communications with Bogotá, and like a fool I believed both Pedro and them.

This excellent communication is a transmitter upon which Pedro, by violently pedaling a generator, can painfully tap out a message in Morse. He gets it three-quarters right when sober, but invariably transcribes the reply wrong. One can also send a letter or telegram by any launch going up river to the edge of civilization and be assured that it will reach a post office in a week or two.

I suppose I ought to have a radio station of my own,

but I do not want to make too many demands when both the Mission and the Government have been generous already. And I really cannot spare the time to take a short course and learn to handle the thing.

Entirely responsible for my presence here are Mario and his wife Teresa. In my tentative botanical explorations of the meeting of forest and llano I came upon this estancia and observed that Mario, then living in a solid shack built into the debris of the peons' cabins, had created a kitchen garden and was not only growing melons, beans and pimientos but selling them. Bartering would better describe his complicated half-and-half transactions.

I was instantly impressed by this proud agriculturalist among carnivorous llaneros who only dismount to eat and sleep and Indians who scratch the soil for subsistence. I had found my assistant and adviser who at the same time was a caretaker of empty rooms and had a wife to cook and clean.

And for my purposes the place was perfect, allowing me to experiment with wheats and fodders, and with rice around the outlet of the marshes. Most of the known food plants of tropical America can easily be cultivated, as well as a number of unknown collected from the edge of the forest — which I shall find disappointingly cataloged when I return to London in a couple of years.

Mario has the thick, smooth body of the Indian and the mobile, furrowed face of a Spanish peasant. A

throwback. He can have little Spanish blood. He understands what I am doing and talks of remaking the Garden of Eden. On the strength of half a dozen Bible
stories for children he considers himself a gallant Catholic. There is no church within a hundred miles, but I
hear that a priest has been known to visit Santa Eulalia
to solemnize marriages and baptize children.

Teresa — well, what is Teresa? Gentle, brown, with
deep, sagging wrinkles and dirty, pendulous breasts. A
caricature of the female body, though she cannot yet be
forty. She bore three boys in her teens and accepts that
she is unlikely to see any of them again: simple laborers vanished into the continent. Every man to her is a
son. My clothes are crudely mended. My tastes are studied so far as raw material permits. There is plenty of
room for culinary experiment even if most food is
grilled over the ashes or stewed in a black pot.

She came up as a girl from Brazil and speaks a mixture of Portuguese and Spanish. She cannot describe
how she came or why. None of the forest people has
much idea of geography. Any long journey is up and
down rivers, and by the time you reach your destination
you may have traveled to every point of the compass.
Thus the mental map of anyone who cannot read a
printed map is very odd indeed. If the sense of locality
belonging to a million fish could be compounded into
one brain, it would be somewhere near Teresa's picture
of her world.

The llaneros of course have a normal picture. Their

horizon may be bounded by the precipice of the forest, by high stands of rushes or by a flickering of palms in the haze, but it is usually circular. The sun moves unclouded. East and west are fixed. Few llaneros can read, but all can understand a map — since their world is flat — and can mark accurately vegetation which might be of interest to me.

The next individual in order of importance is Pedro, the headman of Santa Eulalia, who represents Government in that he has stamps to sell to anyone who can write a letter. He has authority to arrest — though he has no prison — and to commandeer river transport which means an Indian and a canoe. He also keeps the village store and some pigs. When he kills one, I have to buy pork for the sake of his goodwill but often bury it as unfit to eat. It is unnecessary to swear Teresa to silence. Her manners are courtly by nature.

Pedro was a corporal in the army, and perhaps a quarter of his blood is Spanish. He would be better with less, being too inclined to pointless eloquence. He is short, dark, with a wide, slack mouth and a sprinkling of hairs on the upper lip. He gains face from his intimacy with the Misionero and is pleasant enough when I swallow his abominable spirits in his company.

Santa Eulalia itself consists of some twenty mud-and-bamboo huts on a track which leads up from the river crossed by one short, dusty street with the infinity of the llanos at each end of it. We call the intersection the Plaza because it has a tree, the remains of a seat and

Pedro's store. The majority of the inhabitants are llaneros who once worked for the estancia. Others are just
nomads who drifted in. There are also a few families of
pure Indians permanently camped in the woodland
along the river and gathering more food than they
grow. There is so little money in circulation that three
times the same unmistakable coin has been given to me
in change.

Now, what is there in this primitive and friendly society which does not make sense? I will start with the
simple fact — there are others less simple — that I can
never be sure why the estancia was deserted. Mario,
Pedro and the rest vary the reasons they give me and
forget what they have said.

Ownership is of the vaguest. Mario has a bit of paper,
signed by one Manuel Cisneros, giving him the right to
the house and its enclosed garden for as long as he
likes. Cisneros, he tells me, was a Venezuelan who undoubtedly possessed the deeds and brought down his
men and cattle across the plains. He had a sun-crazed
dream of driving herds up to Bogotá on the hoof. When
he found he couldn't he deserted the place, vanished
into the rivers and has never been heard of since. His
capital investment was small and probably never regis-
tered. I think he merely added some adobe and timber
to the ruins of the ancient house and branded a lot
more cattle which belonged to nobody. God knows
where and from whom he bought the place! I tried to

find some record of him in Bogotá, but there was nothing.

This ghostly ownership is in itself slightly disturbing to modern man. We all live like Indians without any title but custom, floating upon a sea of grass which does not lend itself to precise boundaries of social relationship. We and our horses have just enough to eat. We keep our mouths shut if we see what we are not supposed to see, and we are rather too ready to imagine what we don't see. We tend to die young from violence or accident, but general health is good, far better than in the forest. Our medicine man, Joaquín, is a specialist in tropical diseases. His remedies are more effective and his incantations more impressive than those of, say, eighteenth-century doctors. He and I are at present conducting a series of experiments — a leisure activity marked for amusement only —to see whether rhythmic prayer has any measurable effect on growth. Our preliminary results seem to show an increase of eleven per cent in cereal germination, but I must devise a more refined technique for ruling out coincidence.

That is by the way. An example just to remind me that I can and do enjoy myself. I find no lack of personal solidity in this dream life. What I want is to define the other men who share it with me. Difficult, of course. Even Freud could not analyze the motives of one's companions in a dream, only of the dreamer. These people are courteous, trusting and quite intelligent enough to understand my objectives; so there should be no mysteries. Yet they are haunted by a something which they never talk about to me and rarely, I suspect, among themselves. For want of a better theory I shall assume they collectively murdered Manuel Cisneros for good reasons of their own, but put it out that he had taken to the other darkness and might some day return, unobtrusively as he had come, by way of the Orinoco or the Amazon.

[*March 15, Tuesday*]

On Sunday one of the Intendencia's light aircraft came in with mail, some hormone weed killer which I badly needed, sacks of phosphate, a new microscope and a dozen bottles of Scotch with the compliments of the Administration. A civil, kindly lot they are! It would be so easy to forget about me and leave me to be supplied by pack horse or the Government Canoe. Yet if I have any urgent needs and a plane can reasonably be diverted, down it comes within a mile of the estancia. At the end of the wet season when the grass was long I was limited to rare landings on the river.

The plane also brought me a guitar. It seems incredible that in Santa Eulalia there is not a single guitar. Our remoteness does not account for it. The reason, I think, is that at bottom we are still primitive, horse-riding Indians. Although we speak Castilian and call ourselves Christians the music of the Conquerors is not essential to us. So Santa Eulalia's one guitar was allowed to rot away some years ago. That shows how marginal is our Spanish-American culture. A guitar ought to be one of the simple necessaries of life along with salt, pimientos and alcohol.

Yesterday I slung it on my back like a traveling minstrel and rode Tesoro over to Santa Eulalia in the cool of the evening. I play with more emotion than accuracy and can easily improvise words and accompaniment when memory fails. It is astonishing that the English ever accepted the fashion of writing poetry in rhyme. To find rhymes in a Latin language is effortless and spontaneous, and so laborious a task in ours.

The males of Santa Eulalia collected immediately around Pedro's store, crammed on his two benches or squatting more comfortably in the dust. Inevitably he sold more of his rotgut than the public could easily afford. Upon me, too, it was forced, as if Spanish music compelled an exaggerated imitation of Spanish hospitality. I had to drink more than I wanted, but by shifting my position so that I was outside the circle of the single paraffin lamp I was able to spill a glass or two on the ground.

When I slipped off to have a pee against the back of Pedro's store — if they held firmly to one culture or the other they would clean it up — Joaquín spoke to me from the darkness. We have great confidence in each other. Natural enough. The shaman and I are the only two people for hundreds of miles who are professionals.

"I have something hard to speak," he remarked.

"Between friends nothing is hard."

"Look! They will all be in debt to Pedro."

That had not occurred to me. Perhaps it should have. Of course my amateur, pseudo-Argentine performance on the guitar was as if a fair had come to town, unprecedented, unprepared for, destructive of the local economy.

Joaquín knew that my percipience was sharpened by alcohol. His own people react more brutally to the drug. With llanero or Indian he would never have embarked on the subject so abruptly. It shows what a close observer of human nature he is, even when foreign to him.

I thanked him warmly and said that I would ride home after giving two more songs for the sake of the party.

"No. I have spread a new hammock for you."

It was pointless to sleep in his hut. I should not be allowed to go to bed for hours if it were known that I was staying the night in Santa Eulalia. I told him that I was honored by his invitation, but that the only way to put an end to the drinking was to ride off.

"Alone?"

"There is a good moon."

"Wait!"

I knew what Joaquín was up to. He was going to arrange an escort of two or three llaneros which in the genial atmosphere would increase to half a dozen.

I would spend more evenings in Santa Eulalia if only I could avoid this ridiculous, noisy cavalcade which always has to accompany me home and then ride the twelve miles back to the settlement, refusing to stay under my hospitable roof — where there is any — till dawn.

They dislike this, however many of them there are. They won't admit it, but they are afraid of night — at any rate in the utterly empty llano between Santa Eulalia and the estancia. In Argentina I found reasonable caution, but not this childish fear. It is due, I suppose, to the proximity of the forest, although the creek and the marshes cut them off from it. These people belong to the open, blazing savannah and are not so familiar with trees as the Brazilians.

So after another song or two I mounted Tesoro without warning, shouted good night and was away before anyone could follow. It was hardly polite, but eccentricity in the otherwise entertaining Misionero will be forgiven.

I rode home without incident wondering about the relations between what one might call Church and State in Santa Eulalia. I came to the conclusion that Joaquín's intervention was odd and exceptional — as if in England the village parson had broken up a session in the village pub — and that he must have had some other reason besides that he gave me. But all one can tell is that Joaquín, in spite of the squalor of his house and person, has an older wisdom and more authority than the traditionless, semiofficial storekeeper.

This morning, during our desultory conversation while collecting grass seeds, I told Mario what had happened. I suspect that he distrusts Pedro, or rather would distrust him if he could bring himself to do so. It is essential to feel on good terms with the only man who buys and sells. What would you do without him?

"He has a good heart," Mario said, "but thinks he knows everything."

"And Joaquín?"

"This is his country."

I saw what he meant. Joaquín and a few families of pure Indian blood were here or hereabouts before Santa Eulalia existed. The other inhabitants just drifted together like random particles collecting in a void to form a raindrop.

"He should not have let you ride alone."

"I gave him no time. One moment there, the next in the darkness. And everyone knows there is not a horse in the village to catch Tesoro."

As if to excuse Joaquín, he mumbled something about there being little danger on the way to the estancia.

"And what danger is there here?" I asked immediately.

He gave the vague answer that a man should never travel without arms. I replied that my rifle would have been useless, that I couldn't have hit the house after all I had been forced to drink.

"Better the guitar!" I added to amuse him. "If the jaguars don't like the tune, they'll run. And if they do, they can dance."

This casual remark had the most surprising effect. He stared at me with his copper face turning yellow.

"Do not even think of it!" he said.

So Mario is afraid of the guitar as well as the dark! Could this be Joaquín's other reason: that he instinctively distrusts so small a tinkle in so much empty silence? I must be more mysterious to them than I have ever guessed, if they think of me as a possible Pied Piper for jaguars.

[*March 17, Thursday*]

When I decided to make this place my field station I was officially warned of possible danger from bandits. There aren't any. They joined the guerrillas in the hope of more regular hours for rations and murder. They will not appreciate Marxist discipline and the leadership of intellectuals; but once in, a man cannot easily get out.

These partisans of the National Liberation Army normally avoid the llanos since any considerable body of men would find no cover from air reconnaissance and attack. All the same, they keep a close watch on this flank from which their strongholds in the Eastern

Cordillera might be threatened. It stands to reason that all activities in this emptiness, including my own, must be of interest.

I have at last had a visit from them. In the late afternoon of yesterday two men rode up to the estancia, dressed as forest travelers rather than llaneros and speaking cultivated Spanish. Following the custom of the country, I told them that my house was theirs for as long as they cared to honor it and I laid on drinks in the shade.

One was much taller than the other and, I should say, a Colombian of pure Spanish descent. I did not recognize the accent of his companion. He had some Negro blood and may have been a Cuban. Neither of them had the proper air of being born on horseback. They could ride all right, but might have borrowed their two weary beasts for a week's holiday.

Before darkness set in I showed them over our extensions to Mario's garden, the new experimental plots and my field laboratory, explaining the purely advisory role of the Mission. I told them that someday the Government would undertake — or have the pious intention of undertaking — vast schemes of education and colonization, but that for many years to come the only farmers would be experts like myself.

The Cuban — if he was one — seemed to me somewhat naïve, as Spanish-American idealists often are. I could almost hear him thinking whether it was possible

that tropical agriculture could be cover for some operation of the CIA. A pitiless, malignant bunch they are by
all accounts, and no less credulous when it comes to
politics!

When we had settled down again indoors, this
smaller fellow started to cross-examine me. Where had
I learned Spanish? I told him that I was born and bred
in Argentina where my father had been a railway man-
ager until we were thrown out. All my university education had been in England and I had opted for British
nationality; but I had never lost my liking for the Americas.

Some of the subsequent conversation I shall try to
give verbatim, for I might want to refer to it.

"Is it American or British capital behind you?" he
asked.

I explained that there was no private capital whatever behind the Mission and that we were simply putting our technical expertise at the disposal of the Colombian Government.

"To prevent revolution?"

I replied that I didn't give a damn about revolution,
that communist dictatorship was a crude, sure way of
developing virgin territory, but that I thought it an unnecessary discipline for viable economies.

"Good enough for the peon, but not for the British?"

Brash irony! It was time to put him in his place.

"Exactly. Like that plow you saw out there. A British

farmer would have no use for it whatever. But it's cheap, and a vast improvement on anything the Indian villagers ever had."

The Colombian was, I think, inclined to enjoy this confrontation between his opinionated companion and myself, but did not wish it to go too far. I wonder which of them will eventually bump the other off.

"You are not afraid to be alone here?" he asked.

"No. My interest is in agriculture, not politics. And I keep my mouth shut."

"What would you have to open it about?"

I thought it wise that all our cards should be on the table.

"Gentlemen, would I be right to assume that you have called on me in order to decide whether my throat is worth cutting or not?"

They protested most politely against the thought of such brutality towards a generous and sympathetic host, but admitted that up in the Cordillera my doings had attracted curiosity.

"Do believe me, my distinguished friend, this talk of throat-cutting is quite fantastic," the Colombian said. "I recognize that you are giving highly valuable, essential service to my country."

I was not going to be sidetracked by civility. I wanted to be certain, once and for all, that there would be no interference with my work. So I lectured them bluntly. It went against the grain, but I knew they would expect frankness from an Englishman. One must sometimes live up to a false reputation in order to be trusted.

I emphasized that agitated speculation about what I knew and what I didn't could be dangerous to us all and a waste of time; and I went on in some such words as these:

"Using plain common sense — for I have no military knowledge — it has occurred to me that your partisans must eat and that the llaneros have for the moment a market. I am not asking you to tell me whether I am right. I only want you to feel secure if I have visitors from the Army or the Intendencia, as any time I might. I offer you silence on condition that I am left in peace to get on with my work."

The Cuban listened to all this as if he were longing to slice me open and search for truth in my bowels. The Colombian's eyes were flickering with amusement.

"What an excellent intelligence officer you would make!" he said. "But do you think you would notice this supposed movement to market?"

"No. The only route would be north of the marshes. And they don't like grazing cattle even there."

"So the presence of cattle would be exceptional and worth reporting," the Cuban declared.

Pedro must have put them on to this. If he could persuade the llaneros to drive a herd round the marshes, they could then continue on, through parkland providing easy going and patches of cover, right to the foot of the Cordillera.

I asked the Cuban with some contempt whether he

thought I was prepared to spend weeks on horseback with a pair of field glasses for the sake of political convictions or a hundred pesos' reward.

The Colombian waved him down — in fact, back into his chair.

"This is all conjecture," he said. "But I observe, doctor, that you are not accustomed to control your curiosity. Please do so! You might find yourself involved in reprisals against Santa Eulalia, and then it would be hard to guarantee your life. Or you might have to jump on the first boat back to Liverpool."

I replied that I was not going to be scared out of work which I enjoyed.

"Forcibly deported was what I meant," he answered. "It would be easy to convince the Government that you are on our side. You're an intellectual, you see. And policemen always consider that the sympathies of an intellectual must be far to the left. Very odd, but there it is!"

He was still amused and cordial. We might have been at a café table with an old waiter hovering around and smiling discreetly at the talk. I don't see how these fellows can mix a sense of comedy with a cold disregard of human life. That comes naturally to the gaucho or llanero, but their disregard is not cold; it is hot and passionate.

"Then may I assume that my life, my guns and my horses will remain with me?"

"Of course! Why not? And we shall hope someday to employ so sympathetic a character."

"I can't speak Chinese."

"You revolt me, brother! What's for dinner?"

"Stuffed pimientos and a roast."

"By God, you're lucky round here!" the Cuban exclaimed, greed or hunger breaking his startled silence. "Well, no more politics — and be at ease!"

Thereafter their relaxation was genuine. We did not, however, arrive at any convivial relationship. It stands to reason that they were not so eager for companionship as I. They probably longed for privacy and for freedom from the unending duty to their troops. Still, I could sleep soundly and I hope they did.

They were off at dawn after a cup of coffee. The Colombian, before he left, took me to the corral on the excuse that his horse's pastern was cut. On examination I found little or no damage. It was clear that he wanted to talk confidentially.

"I don't understand the llaneros," he said. "Few of us do. Are they much influenced by superstition?"

Every llanero would declare himself a good Catholic, devoted to the Virgin and the Saints. But since he rarely rides so far as a church and there are few missionaries to correct his errors, what he really worships and fears is a Mother Goddess with her attendant spirits. Even so he is less influenced by superstition than the settled Indians who know just enough Christianity to have lost respect for their own myths. The human longing for faith goes unfulfilled in both, leaving a void through which writhe the misty fears of spirits, the dead and magic. Joaquín at least hangs on to his old traditions, but is unable to explain what he really does believe.

Even Mario and Teresa are afraid of duendes. When I settled in, they moved from their cabin over to the main building. Their excuse was that they could serve me better if they lived alongside. It sounded reasonable; but I am certain, now that I know them better, that the true reason was reluctance to walk the couple of hundred yards across the garden after sunset.

So I told the Colombian that, whatever the superstitions, they were not Christian and would still be alive even if he and his party succeeded in closing every church in the country.

"Why are there no cattle between Santa Eulalia and your estancia?" he asked.

"I wish I knew. They think the grazing unlucky rather than unhealthy."

"And Pedro? Does he share this belief?"

"Pedro either thinks he knows or is content to be ignorant. An old soldier with no imagination at all."

"It seems useless to ask why in this country," he said.

"It isn't useless, but there is hardly ever any answer. That's what I wanted to explain to your companion last night. To whom should I talk and what evidence would I have? He didn't realize the emptiness. All one notices is a speck on the horizon or a dance of the dust which might be haze, perhaps a horseman."

"You wrote something like that when the Mission questioned your choice of this station," he said. "You insisted that the first object of study should be the ecology of fertile soil uncontaminated by man."

I exclaimed that surely he couldn't get hold of copies of the Mission's reports to the Department of Agriculture.

"Only the first," he replied. "I was much impressed by your contribution. Indeed I thought this visit to you quite unnecessary. But my companion is not accustomed to judge by internal evidence. He has not that sort of education."

Well, I suppose it is not surprising that these able and misguided fellows who take to the mountains should keep a line open to former colleagues in the administration. Evidently he has no great respect for his lieutenant. It's my guess that the Cuban is their chief of security. All chiefs of security are, inevitably and by profession, bastards. I had better control my curiosity and go on minding my own business whether in Santa Eulalia or Bogotá.

[*March 20, Sunday*]

The heat is windless and silent, illimitable as daylight on the moon. Nothing moves until an hour before sunset when again one hears the birds on the marshes and the monkeys howling at the edge of the forest.

The herds, split up into small, languid bunches, are far out in the llano or in the shade of the woodland close to Santa Eulalia along the Guaviare. The llaneros are weary of their half-starved, tireless horses and ride no more than they must to see what casualties, if any, there are among the resting cattle. Losses are few. Puma in the open or jaguar on the edge of cover must be bold and hungry to tackle these formidable, half wild beasts and are likely to be trampled into a bag of empty skin. Near water the anaconda is the worst enemy. These giant constrictors kill seldom, but a young animal has no chance against them. The llaneros swear that an anaconda can pulp the life out of a full-grown bull but is unable to swallow it.

Among my other reasons for the choice of the estancia was its unfailing water supply. According to Mario, Pedro and Joaquín the chain of marshes and the nameless creek which drains them never dry. I hope not, but the rains ended a month too soon. The creek is a necklace of pools linked by shallows and the level of the marshes has sunk.

The *acequías* which irrigate our garden have little water in them. They must be deepened and extended, but Mario and I alone cannot do it. Labor is unobtainable. The few available Indians of Santa Eulalia, suspended in almost complete idleness, will not work through the heat of the day — for which I don't blame them — cannot be induced to leave their wretched huts to live here, will not ride the twelve miles and return.

Nor can I get llaneros, whatever pay I offer. They are the last of the world's horsemen, now that the Mongols have taken to cities and the Bedouin to oil and education. It would be beneath their dignity to work in a field. I never even see a solitary rider on the skyline who might welcome a change from his futile life of producing valueless, ownerless beef.

So there we are! In this exceptional drought a lot of my work is going for nothing, since I cannot get enough water to the parched crops. I have tried the primitive device of a balanced pole, leather bucket and counterweight. It works and my carpentry was fun, but the labor of raising and tipping water is endless and intolerable. Thank God the horses and ourselves have an inexhaustible supply from the deep well in the courtyard!

I could not persuade Mario to show interest in my hydraulics. Unless I keep him working in my sight he insists on stopping holes and breaches in our ruinous adobe wall. It is good enough to keep out cattle, which don't come here anyway, but it will not, he says, keep out deer. That's true enough, and it might be wise, before the rains, to have some wire flown in to top the wall. Mario has never seen a wire fence and could not understand it until I drew a picture for him. He then assured me it would be useless. He is obsessed by a vision of deer crawling underneath the wire, which is

[35]

preposterous. To listen to Mario, one might think this country was swarming with game, all eager to eat up experimental crops and not in the least afraid of human settlement. I think I am again faced by the blank — evasive and at present unmeaning.

[*March 22, Tuesday*]

Alarums and Excursions! Santa Eulalia has been reminded that it is governed.

Normally we have no Government, unless one counts Pedro. We have neither education nor police nor public works on which to spend money, and no property or income on which to raise it. Since there is nothing worth stealing, there is no crime but manslaughter. One cannot call it murder, for there is no intent to kill. One gentleman decides that the words or eyes of another are offensive. As they may have one-eighth of Spaniard between them and an ancient tradition of violence while in liquor, they slash at one another with their knives. A pint or two of blood is mopped up. Its former owner quickly replaces it or dies. First aid is administered by Joaquín. The affair is recorded by Pedro. That is all.

Well, as I say, Government has intruded upon our peace. The first I knew of it was a yellow haze which resolved itself into half a dozen men riding up to the estancia — on borrowed horses since they had arrived at Santa Eulalia by a military launch.

[36]

The cavalcade consisted of a captain, a sergeant, three men and an unwilling guide. It never occurred to me before that strangers might need one. The tracks are little used and deceptive. Neither I nor my few visitors follow the same path except in the wet season. We may come in from any point on a semicircle of nothing.

That evening we had little but our homegrown vegetables and canned meat — of which they would all be heartily sick. So as soon as Mario and the guide had seen to the horses and I had exaggeratedly welcomed the party, I told their Captain that it was not too late for some duck if we hurried.

He jumped at the opportunity, and I sent him up the marsh with instructions to show himself on the shore of an inlet where the birds were just beginning to settle. They did what I expected, changing direction and circling low over the pools and rushes at the mouth of the creek. The light had nearly gone, but the flighting duck were black against the vivid green of the western sky and it was one of those memorable evenings when I was shooting like the angel of death. Fifteen duck with sixteen cartridges and all dropped where I could get at them!

Meanwhile the sergeant and his men had gathered in the kitchen and their horses were tethered to the old hitching posts outside. Mario and the guide were obstinately reluctant to leave them there, but I would not have them in the corral with my own. I am prepared to put up one or, at a pinch, two when passers-by stay the

[37]

night, but I drew the line at crowding six into the small enclosure with possible damage to Tesoro, Estrellera and the sun shelters.

"And if they break loose into the garden?" Mario asked.

"Well, hobble them and turn them out onto the llano. They can come to no harm," I said.

But perhaps I should not be as free and easy here as in Argentina. Pumas do range over the llanos, though I have never seen one. And a horse unaccustomed to marshes might go unwarily into the water over his knees and land himself in trouble with electric eel or sting ray. No shortage of those sods!

"For the honor of the house a horse must not be lost," Mario insisted. "I shall put them, if the master permits, in the hall."

I shrugged my shoulders and told him to go ahead. The hall is a ruin with hardly any roof, but it has four stout walls, a solid door and shuttered windows.

While the rest of the party were drinking rotgut and helping Teresa to pluck the duck, Captain Valera and I opened up the whisky which the Administration had sent me — presumably knowing that I might have visitors and wishing to reinforce my goodwill. I found Valera a delightful and intelligent companion. He had chosen to serve in the vast wastelands of Colombia and was supported in discomfort and hardship by a vision of what his country could become. He was the type of idealist who might well have joined the revolutionaries in the Cordillera, but he loathed them and their methods. They might, he admitted, bring more social justice to the Indian and the laborer, but then would stick fast in the mess of their doctrinaire economics, and take fifty years, like the Russians, to arrive at the same point that Western democracies had reached in thirty.

He knew all about the Mission and was enthusiastic over what he called my self-sacrifice. I explained that I hadn't any, that in me scientific curiosity took the place of patriotism in him. We were both doing what we most wanted to do.

"And what about women?" he asked. "Forgive me — but I don't see one."

I replied that I was not too sure of Government regulations. Laws for the protection of the Indians did exist, though they were somewhat starry-eyed and unenforceable. So I preferred to avoid illegalities which could be used against me if anyone wanted to stop my work.

I may have sounded prim, and he smiled at what he thought typical Englishness.

"I wonder Mario and Teresa haven't shoved something in your bed already," he said.

"It would have to be pitch dark," I answered. "The only possible candidate has not much nose left."

He said that he might be able to do better for me than that. If I didn't like it, I could return it by Government Canoe. He would let me know.

I hope he does nothing of the sort. The casual way in which Latin Americans pass secondhand females to each other is inclined to inhibit desire. As soon as the rains come, I shall fly up to Bogotá and fornicate more artistically.

Teresa was using her longest spit for the duck and needed wood as well as charcoal, so we had to wait some time for our meal. Meanwhile Valera opened up the subject of his visit.

It appeared that guerilla activity had been spotted from the air before the commando could disperse and vanish into the foothills. The General Staff was not in the least bothered about an advance southeastwards in our direction which could get nowhere and occupy nothing. The guerrilleros might as well put out to sea. But since they had never come down to the llanos before Military Intelligence was curious.

So Valera had been ordered to ask questions wherever there was any articulate soul along the banks of the Guaviare to answer them. He had called at Santa Eulalia and talked to Pedro, who had denied any knowledge of guerrilleros but had spoken of the mysterious doings of the Englishman at the estancia and his unknown visitors.

I said that I did very occasionally give hospitality to travelers who might be Marxists or horse thieves or Venezuelans on the run for all I knew. It was the custom in Argentina to keep open house and ask no questions, and I presumed that Colombian courtesies were the same.

That satisfied Valera. After all, no one could talk to

me for long without realizing that I have no politics. I was determined not to mention my suspicions of the llaneros' cattle market. I shall not give away Valera's secrets either.

While we ate he told me plenty. His second task was to report on whether a small, airborne force could attack from this side and startle the revolutionaries into retiring further north where troops from Bogotá could get at them. After returning to his temporary headquarters he intended to do some mapping with this operation in mind. I advised him to leave his mapping for another month when the rains would reveal unexpected lakes and creeks. I could imagine his handful of troops boldly attacking some guerrilla outpost and finding too late that there was a sluggish river hidden in a fold of the ground.

He asked why I suspected that there was any guerrilla activity so far east. I could only answer that Pedro and the llaneros had told me so.

"That's a lot more than they ever told me," he said.

I was saved from what might have been awkward interrogation by Mario and Teresa coming in to clear away and to report that the troops had gone over to their former cabin for the night.

Across the garden I could hear singing and general jollity. A red glow suspended in blackness showed that the five men had started to grill a second supper in the chimney. I knew that they had a plentiful supply of rum to go with it. It seemed a pity that Mario and

Teresa, whose life was so lonely, should not join the party.

"Can any of your fellows play a guitar?" I asked Valera.

"My sergeant. Like an angel."

I told Mario to drop everything and take Teresa and my guitar over to the other side of the garden, leaving us to look after ourselves.

He would not, though I could see he longed to. I was exasperated by his fear of the dark.

"Look, friend Mario, there are no duendes who can stand an electric torch!" I exclaimed. "It is as good as the Sign of the Cross. I will see you both over to your old house."

He sulked but had to agree. Valera came as well, assuring him that duendes invariably respected his rank and uniform.

We stayed long enough to listen to a song and then relieved them of our presence so that they would be less inhibited. Teresa, as befitted a respectable matron, had withdrawn to the doorway of the next room — a shawl-shrouded figure with a black grin. Mario was becoming noisy. It was clear that I had done the right thing.

"Why wouldn't they go?" Valera asked when we had settled down for a last whisky before turning in. "Snakes? Or is this place haunted?"

I was surprised that he should accept the possibility so naturally. But he had an open mind and he probably knew deserted plantations on the riverbanks where

[42]

there is something one might call an aura of despair and death.

"Not in the least. Thoroughly cheerful," I said. "It must be the result of their loneliness before I came. In the forest I should not blame Mario. If a man is superstitious and cannot put a name to the night sounds, there is no place which is not haunted."

"But here —" he made a magnificent Latin gesture to describe emptiness and knocked his glass over "— we have no companions but the stars."

"That's what I feel myself," I answered. "The forest is on our doorstep but we are not of it. Like a cinema screen. So near, so different a life, such limited values. And we observe it all from our seats."

I was pleased with that. I usually approach truth through wine, not whisky.

This morning they rode back to Santa Eulalia. Valera intends to return to his headquarters and then run up to Bogotá to report. I think his party should travel in civilian dress, but they will all flaunt their uniforms. I know nothing of the military art, but personally I should never employ a Latin American on any secret mission. I wonder if the National Liberation Army can do better. Perhaps that is one of the ingredients of such success as they have.

[43]

[*March 23, Wednesday*]

Today I rode Estrellera over to Santa Eulalia and spent an hour or two with Pedro — ostensibly to buy rice and cans of sardines of which Mario and Teresa are very fond. Shortage of fats, probably. I have seen Teresa with an oily sardine in one hand and a sticky sweet in the other, quivering with delight at the sensation in her potbelly and regardless of the mess on her face.

Pedro is a curious character, fairly honest and utterly unimaginative — the typical corporal. One could not wish for a more useful companion in forest or on the llano; if there was anything edible about, he would climb for it, shoot it or dig it out. But it would be hard to stand his continual chatter. I should get so tired of the rise and fall of his scanty moustache that I should be tempted to pay him to shave it off. He would, too — on condition that everyone believed he had done it to please me and not for money.

Money. He'll need two crates to carry it to the bank when he retires: filthy little bits of paper and packets of small change. As a favor to him I took a sack of the stuff with me the last time I flew to Bogotá. He is not a miser. He knows what interest is, but wouldn't dream of charging it on debts at the store and small loans. He has not the aimlessness of his fellow citizens. He intends to buy a bar in some poor but honest quarter of Bogotá.

[44]

His wife looks after his capital and hides it away in small flour bags, reciting a spell over every cache. She is a pure Indian who never says much. She wouldn't have a chance anyway, since Pedro uses her as an audience when he can't find a better. All their children died young. On these over-violent llanos death in one's twenties is more common.

The store was empty. It always is till evening. Over the second rotgut Pedro said to me dramatically:

"One of these days I shall pop a shot in my head."

He never will, but the fact that he can say it separates him from Indians and llaneros. For them suicide is just as impossible as for an animal. Their business is to live. They have no other.

"And why is that, friend?" I asked.

"Politics."

"They don't concern us here. Did Captain Valera want you to go along with him?"

No, no, he insisted. As the agent of Government he was too valuable where he was. A gallant officer such as Captain Valera knew the worth of a reliable ex-corporal at his post.

I think it likely that Valera was taken in. Pedro can play the old soldier very well. But I know that he is at least on speaking terms with guerrilla leaders, and that he tried to suggest the estancia as the cause of any rumors that Valera might have heard.

In view of what goes on at his store, his nerves ought to be proof against anything. But he is never in personal danger. He *is* Santa Eulalia. Without him it would have no official existence. Put it this way. Footballers assault each other, but not the referee. They are aware that if they had no referee, they would be left with only a field: a small, dull, flat llano.

So Pedro's courage — unquestionable in matters of survival and sheer endurance — has never been tested by worries. With one hand he performed his minimal duties to the State; with the other he took a small subvention from the guerrillas. It looked as if that could go on forever in his apathetic world. Valera's appearance was unexpected and alarming.

"What do you think?" he asked. "Who is going to win?"

"The Government, of course. There are only a hundred of the others."

"But more can come from Cuba. Where is this Cuba exactly?"

"An island twelve hundred miles away."

"It is said that everyone is equal there."

"So we are here."

"But in the cities, too, over there. Think of it, friend! If the guerrillas capture Bogotá they will give money to the poor so that everyone is equal."

He was off. He drew an eloquent picture of Utopia which I swear must have been influenced by some army chaplain's description of the joys of heaven. He left out harps and glassy sea, but gave me a clear impression of a smiling population sitting around listening to brass bands while shining Pedros marched up and down the main street. This stuff could certainly tickle the imaginations of the submerged Indian peons, release from hell in this life being a more substantial promise than release from hell in the next. By giving food to the partisans as well as money to the priests one could take out real comprehensive insurance.

"But do you believe it, Pedro?" I asked.

"I? Not I! There will always be rich and poor, officers and men."

That was not put on to impress me with his loyalty to the Government. It was his sincere common-sense opinion. The world's middle class of corporals distrust revolution.

"Then what are you worrying about?"

"Such cruelty! They take no prisoners, shooting them in the back and cutting their throats and worse! Crucifying them with their toes in an ant's nest! Making them sit on sharp bamboos till at last the end comes out of their mouths!"

He was away again — more ants, alligators, skinning with blunt machetes, anything he could think of.

I knew very well that while he was talking about prisoners he was thinking of traitors. So I reinforced his neutrality by assuring him that the army was just as cruel. I doubt if it is, except in rare cases of revenge. I also suspect that most of the rumors of guerrilla atroci-

[47]

ties are set going by themselves. More borrowings from the Church. Threaten the opposition with devils, fire and pitchforks, and they'll behave!

"Thank God I do not mix myself in their quarrels!" he said. "And I advise you not to. I, Pedro, advise you."

"Me? I'm a Government servant! With the friends I have in high places in Bogotá it would be quite impossible."

So it is. But I reserve the right to talk to guerrilleros if I want to until such time as they are deservedly wiped out. In a village — a true, tiled village — of the Cordillera that might be irresponsible. But here any humanity is welcome. Neither politics nor religion can override the claims of hospitality.

"You will tell your friends when you go to Bogotá?" Pedro asked anxiously. "You will tell them that I think only of my duty?"

Poor Pedro! Being questioned by Valera has let in the blank. I wonder how far he has committed himself. My guess is that he merely told a few of the wilder llaneros that if they were to drive cattle to some known landmark they wouldn't be the worse for it.

The llaneros live as best they can. The right way to look at them is not as cattlemen at all, but as hunters and conservers of semi-wild beasts. Since they have not received any wages for years they keep going by eating beef and rather reluctantly supplying — over vast distances — small herds to anyone who will pay cash. The identity of the customer does not interest them. Pedro could plead absolute ignorance that the cattle were being sold to guerrillas. The trouble is that nobody would believe him for long.

I took my siesta in one of his filthy basket chairs. It was twice as hot under his tiled roof — the only one in Santa Eulalia — as under the usual thick thatch. At last I left him sleeping to go and see Joaquín. I wanted to ask him when he thought the rains would come.

Joaquín was peacefully smoking a home-made cigar. His perfectly expressionless eyes were fixed on the water lapping against the jetty of rotten piles where goods are landed — if they don't fall through. By looking closely one could just tell that life flowed in the river and the man.

I laid down on the floor of his hut a few presents from Pedro's store which were very properly ignored. We chatted about neighbors until it was permissible to come to the point. Then he told me that the drought would get worse before it got better, and that he had never known anything like it for twelve years.

"That would be when the estancia was abandoned?" I asked.

"Yes. Twelve years ago."

"And before that?"

"The rains always came in time."

"Can you make them come?"

"Can you?"

He did not understand what I meant. Tropical rains are normally so regular that rainmakers have no market. To set up in business one needs a less reliable climate where a witch doctor can make a reasonable forecast on the strength of weather experience handed down from father to son. Presumably there is nothing more to it.

"There is more I want to ask you, Joaquín," I said. "I must have hands to help me, but no one will come out from Santa Eulalia. Are there any Indians west of the estancia who would work for me?"

"The forest has no men in it."

"And on the other bank of the Guaviare?"

"Too far. They would not come."

Well, that was that. No offer will persuade a tribal Indian to do what he doesn't want to do, or to admit that he won't. He will reply that of course he is coming and that he will send his brother and cousin at once. But none of them ever turns up.

Joaquín's flat statement that the forest beyond the estancia is uninhabited lets in the blank. I used the phrase just now of Pedro. It's obsessive. We are able, when in good spirits, to preserve the self in a solid piece; but if anything disturbs this integrity we expand into nothingness. Alcohol is a cure, and the llaneros give themselves to it as I suspect they do to a woman: very quickly and then to sleep. Myself, when the drought or the absurd fencing or my sheer inability to extract straight answers to straight questions, gets me down, I feel that the gift of speech is useless and wish that I could revel in the nothingness like my ancestor, the running ape, when he first broke out from the crowded darkness of the trees.

Mario and Teresa must have been living the most lonely life imaginable before I came. No wonder he needs a wall around him. A wall drives man and wife back on themselves, giving an illusion of solidarity and safety. So night, when no wall can be seen, is a sort of deprivation. Night forces him into unity with his environment, whereas his life is only tolerable if he can keep his environment at bay.

Amateur psychology, but I can't be far off the truth. Obviously it was a drought twelve years ago that finally finished Manuel Cisneros, the enterprising Venezuelan. I never quite grasped that before. Mario ought to have told me. Naturally he did not. He might have frightened off the boss-companion who had dropped from heaven to make his life more normal. Or am I unjust? He always had enough water for his own surprisingly sophisticated garden and had no reason to suppose there would not be enough for me.

Joaquín and I strolled back to the store to collect Estrellera. She does not care for Pedro, who is too noisy and military, but she always touches muzzles with Joaquín though he never brings her anything to eat. He would make a good vet, if anyone here ever bothered with more than centuries-old bleedings, dosings and cauterization. Such practice as he has is confined to Indian pets: monkeys, agoutis and a variety of small creatures and large birds. His diagnosis is absurd but

his sympathy is genuine. For him we are all spirits confined in flesh.

So I rode home, night falling when I was half way.
Estrellera has no nerves. She will give a snort of indignation at the unfamiliar like any conservative female,
but she never shies, stops dead or trembles. If I were a
guerrillero I think I would prefer to ride the too-alert
Tesoro, but for a journey on which dangers are, I hope,
only imagined, give me Estrellera every time!

[*March 25, Friday*]

A day of paperwork. It was about time that I made a
précis of my journal and sent up a report to Bogotá, if
only to show that I have zealously obeyed my instructions. All experiments of any importance I have initi-
ated myself, disguising such undepartmental enterprise
under a respectful amount of paper in triplicate — very
necessary when the termites may get it if only in dupli-
cate.

The director is most reasonable, partly because I'm
his showpiece. When politicians suggest that we and
our like merely sit on our backsides, with an iced drink
in one hand while the other explores the frilly intima-
cies of Latin-American womanhood, all at the expense
of the Ministry of Overseas Development, he can always point to his field officer slapping mosquitoes in the
dark heart of the continent.

In fact the habitable rooms are often free of insects

and at times cool. When I took possession I repaired all fly screens on the barred north windows facing the courtyard and left the south windows as they were, permanently closed by heavy wooden shutters. Mario advised this on the grounds of keeping out the sun when he really meant the night.

No doubt I sound a much more romantic figure than I am. I have comfortable and modern camp equipment, a sufficiency of medical supplies, a well-stocked bar, all the apparatus I require and a minitractor which is the wonder of the district and in the drought is used for giving rides to visitors. I have even a refrigerator, powered by a small petrol-engined dynamo which supplies enough voltage for half a dozen light bulbs as well.

I prefer living on the country to tinned food. That's where the Americans go wrong. They stock up with cans of rations as tasteless as they are luxurious. You can never really get the feel of an agricultural economy unless you surrender to it. Satisfying my own wants is an essential, additional experiment. Besides the eternal bananas and rice, I have vegetables, eggs, fresh beef and unlimited game. My dear Eibar-made 16-bore keeps me supplied with any size of wildfowl I fancy from snipe to geese, and I picked up in Barranquilla an old British Army Lee-Enfield in excellent condition which produces the occasional deer or peccary for the pot.

No, I do myself pretty well. Admittedly the tropical evenings are long, but I pass them reading or playing records (I never can do both simultaneously) or devising a few experiments so unlikely to succeed that they count as amusement rather than work. This diary helps.

[*March 27, Sunday*]

Tesoro has had a touch of colic. Now that the cracked conduits under the wall are delivering such a wretched flow, he is getting too much sediment in his water. I shall have to draw it from the well.

I was possibly unwise to buy him, for he could not be expected to have the resistance of the native criollos. But I have been amply rewarded. The story goes that some singularly vain captain of Venezuelan cavalry — lousy with oil money — imported a palomino stallion from Mexico which he used as a ceremonial charger to impress the girls. As likely as not it impressed his squadron too. We can none of us resist a touch of lunatic flamboyance.

Tesoro was by this beauty out of a criollo mare. He turned out more gold than dun with the chestnut mane and tail of his dam. I got him cheap, fifteen hands being too big for a cow pony. For polo he wouldn't have a fault, being neat on his legs and of quick intelligence. Indeed I cannot see any faults in him at all, beyond those of youth and very sketchy breaking. When I am on his back he expects severity and does not hold it against me; when I am off it, he follows me about like a dog.

I am always entertained by the marked difference of character between my nervous, affectionate gelding and Estrellera. She got her name from being a stargazer as a filly. It now fits her temperament rather than her conformation. She is inclined to be dreamy with strong likes and dislikes, but all that remains of stargazing is a slight suggestion of a ewe-neck. The llaneros think more highly of her than I do, for she is a typical criollo skewbald of 14.2, well ribbed up and staying forever.

I would not change either of them. With those two horses I would back myself to reach the Orinoco — and that is more than one could do by canoe and still arrive all in one piece.

[*March 31, Thursday*]

I have always assumed that promises will come to nothing — and not only in Latin America. Here, however, the promises have such an air of generous enthusiasm that they are a pleasure in themselves. Fulfilment stuns as a devastating and sometimes embarrassing surprise.

On the twenty-eighth the Government Canoe — more like a barge with an outboard motor — was expected at Santa Eulalia. Since one can never be sure of the exact date of arrival, especially when the Guaviare is low, I

[55]

did not want to waste time hanging about and sent Mario over to deliver and collect my mail.

He returned next day, accompanied by a packhorse loaded with hardware which we needed and, on top of it, an unexpected piece of soft ware. She greeted me very shyly and escaped to Teresa. Mario then presented to me a letter which he had received from an immensely fat and dignified Negress who had insisted on establishing both his identity and mine in the manner of an obstinate sergeant of police. It was from Captain Valera.

My Very Good Friend,

You will have a few weeks in which to get over your surprise before the Canoe calls at Santa Eulalia on the way back. Put her on board if she does not suit, and accept the excuses of a friend who only wished to be of service to you.

First, this is not a whore, merely an unfortunate. My girl, who has a good heart, found it like a stranded fish upon the riverbank. She did not immediately inform me, since it was a good-looking little creature which might have caused some dissension in the family. So she boarded it out for some days until she could settle its future.

When I was about to leave on the little expedition which by good fortune brought me to your house, my girl confessed what she had done. She had to get rid of her find and was afraid that any arrangements made in

[56]

*my absence would come to my ears — as they surely
would — and that I should suspect her of commerce
rather than charity. Her past, I may say, would justify
such suspicion. But her present is in every way loyal
and obliging. Her fears that I might change horses if I
set eyes on Chucha were entirely unfounded.*

*Chucha's history is deplorably vague and unsatisfac-
tory. What else can one expect? A woman is lost among
the insects and the trees. The soul clings to its name in
nameless places and there is no rest for the body.*

*She was given by her mother to a merchant called
Samuel. That regrettable transaction must have taken
place in the Eastern Cordillera of Bolivia or Peru, for
her native language is Aymara. Samuel took her down
to the Amazon basin. After a stay in a large city
where they did not speak Spanish — probably Manaos
— Samuel wandered with her up another river —
probably the Rio Negro. He seems to have been an ir-
repressible traveler, but he was kind to her. He was
drowned somewhere high up the Orinoco. How the devil
he got there from the Rio Negro I don't know, so I can't
expect her to.*

*Chucha, abandoned in the merciless nowhere of our
continent, very reasonably presented her undoubted
charms to the first man who had a boat with an engine
in it — a guarantee that, whatever his appearance, he
was not a forest Indian. His name was Pepe and he
traded in knives, beads and whistles. He was continually drunk and treated her brutally, whereas Samuel*

[57]

offered her no less affection than he gave to his pet monkey.

When Pepe threatened to open her up with a machete she ran away from him. My girl says that the spirit of her great aunt had locked up Chucha's womb. Her own deceased great aunt is, I am glad to say, more reasonable. I must admit that I had no idea that the plateau Indians could suffer from the muscular effects of a neurosis which one believed confined to the women of Northern Europe. She must have been sufficiently exposed to civilization to have acquired taste.

I do not like allowing the poor little thing to die of damp rot complicated by syphilis, and I send her to you with confidence that you will save her from this otherwise inevitable destiny. In the course of various small medical attentions which she badly needed I have had her intimately examined. Indian modesty was appalled, but my girl held her hand and assured her that such was the custom among the rich.

I can certify that when she left here she had no venereal disease, and that during the undoubted hazards of the journey up river she was under the care of a respectable matron whose husband depends on me for promotion.

All I fear is your British sense of responsibility. I beg you to ignore it. You know as well as I do that her relationship with you will greatly enhance her value and that a dowry — tiny to you, wealth to some young llanero — would persuade him to wear out two horses in his immediate search for a priest.

Sentimental cynicism! And barely redeemed by that warmth of friendship which a generous Latin American will allow to blaze on the strength of a single meeting! I reread Valera's letter over a couple of stiff drinks which merely turned one half of me into a rampant stallion while the other half argued. Suppose, I asked myself, this female had been a scientist or some enterprising young woman come from Bogotá to inspect my valuable services to her country? Well, she'd have had to resist attempted rape three times a day, the afternoon attack being marked by the highest fever. Suppose Joaquín had supplied me with something not too jungly from one of the river tribes? I should probably have accepted, since the girl would have a home to which she could return with her presents and be welcome. Chucha had no home. I came to the conclusion that my conscience was bothering me just because she was so helpless. She had no more choice than a mare passed from one llanero to another.

Was all this compunction insincere and did I in fact object to her color? Certainly not! My first inspection of the consignment had been casual, since I had not then read the accompanying Operation Manual. I thought she was possibly some niece of Teresa's. But I found her color delightful — like a new penny set in black,

straight hair rather more luxuriant than that of our
river Indians. She looked neat and clean, except for the
stains of the journey, and no doubt Teresa would de-
louse her if necessary.

Or did I resent being given no choice? No, she would
do very well. I was prepared to put Samuel's little cutie
through the hoops within five minutes and go on till
next Sunday week. So, after all, compunction did appear to be the true motive for hesitation and quite sincere.

I went to Mario's quarters to see her. Mario and Teresa had no doubt what she had come for. They reminded me of a couple of hopeful parents determined
to clear out of the room as soon as possible and leave
future son-in-law to get on with it. They had evidently
been assuring her that I was a nice chap, a mastermind
and so forth. I told Teresa that Chucha would eat with
me and took her along to my living room.

She was very gentle and submissive like most Indian
women, but I preferred to assume that she might have
some elementary pride. So I decided to put off the moment of truth as long as I could without going crazy,
gave her some sweets to suck, showed her round the
habitable rooms and told her a bit about myself and my
work.

She followed me around with blank brown eyes, wide
open. After a while she began to murmur a little chatter. Her Spanish was soft and passable. The white
blouse and skirt that Valera or his girl had dressed her

in were damn near transparent when she had the setting sun behind her. It was time for Sir Galahad to have
another drink just to keep the conversation going.

When I produced bottle and glass she gave her first
sign of being more than a pet monkey with the power of
speech — a little involuntary movement as if she were
shrinking from an outsize spider. I said I never drank
more than a finger — the length of it, not the breadth
— and waggled it at her. I showed her the proportion
of rum and fresh lime juice that I liked and let her play
with the tinkling ice and soda. Confidence was established. She told me that she was about fifteen, that she
was born in Peru but couldn't remember it clearly.

She was very hungry and stuffed herself with beef
and corn as soon as Teresa brought in our meal. She
then was far more talkative. Her father had come down
from the Central Cordillera to the lowlands, having
been selected for one of the Peruvian Government's re-
settlement schemes. That, of course, is my own interpretation of her disconnected bits and pieces. He died
of TB, as far too many of them do when they leave the
winds of the altiplano for the damp and heat, and her
mother carried on working in the plantations. When
she was twelve Samuel and the rivers gathered her up.

"Why didn't you tell all this to the captain and his
señora?" I asked.

"I was afraid."

"What of, child?"

"Of the señora."

"But why?"

"Because she hid me."

I suppose there is some logic in that. Valera's girl created an atmosphere of guilt. Chucha's reaction to it was not unlike that of some city teenager running away from home. To admit exactly where she came from could mean that she would be handed over to the police. She didn't see the Establishment as safety, in which she was instinctively right. The Establishment — if any member of it with a pair of white trousers could be found — would simply have put her on board a canoe in the pious hope that she might reach some nuns and the near certainty that she would not.

Her matt copper had taken on a patina of green. Being fascinated by the quivering of the bell-shaped breasts, I did not notice it until we were near disaster. All those sweets she had eaten were no foundation for an Argentine-sized grill of beef. She was overcome by shame and looked round frantically for somewhere to be sick. Natural good taste or are the Children of the Sun brought up to consider it a disgrace? I don't know. Here we use the open grass or the back of Pedro's store. We also pride ourselves in shooting the contents of our stomachs as far away as possible, regardless of where they land. I suppose she was overwhelmed by a tiled floor, four walls and a table with plates, knives and forks on it. To me it was an indoor camp, but to her the high splendor of a Lord Mayor's banquet.

She made a rush for the nearest window on the outside wall and flung open the wooden shutters. She was very obviously near collapse due to the long weariness of her journey and, perhaps, relief. Relief will often make one more wobbly than the original cause of the strain. She was also in trouble with her hair. So I held her head till she was empty.

I fetched Teresa and explained that Chucha was ill and tired. No doubt Teresa had spotted it much earlier, but had not thought that the master would pay attention. She bedded Chucha down on my spare mattress in an alcove between the kitchen and laboratory and gave her a hot, aromatic tea, possibly more effective than remedies from my medicine chest. Chucha thanked me with great gravity and said she was sorry. So was I.

But I had been rewarded by my first sight of a puma. It must have been crouching very close to the house. However, my eyes had not had time to adjust to the darkness and I only had a vague glimpse of it as it cantered away.

[*April 2, Saturday*]

The next morning she hardly lifted her eyes, but had put a scrap of red ribbon in her hair. She was very attentive to Teresa, learning about a house with walls and how to clean it — all very foreign to her after years of bamboo huts and canoes. She took a little lunch with me and was all "Si, señor" and "No, señor" as if she had just come out of a convent.

[63]

When the house was closed and silent in the heat of the afternoon I gathered her up. She took it very naturally. Well, one would expect that. But I mean a little more by "naturally." There was no immediate, pretended response, nor any of those artificialities which so delightfully disguise a too eager response. She merely hid her face and dissolved into a softness.

I spent a little time and trouble on her. She was nearly passive, except for a slight tremor of muscles which showed that she was not uninterested. There was no trouble due to great aunts. I found her peculiar softness stimulating. It may be due to the fact that like most Indians she has hardly any waist. The little darling had to put up with me from the siesta till dinner time, and soon after that we had the two air mattresses side by side and were off again. For God's sake, what I have been suppressing for the sake of tropical agriculture!

Today I noticed that she was not walking with quite her usual grace. I can't help it. It's going to get sorer before it gets better, like the drought. Her very simple sweetness intoxicates me. She doesn't — or rather didn't — know how to kiss properly. Her minor erotic response is a caress of arms, legs or hands. She ought to have a tail like a cat.

That reminds my one-track mind that she also saw the puma. She was frightened out of her wits and insists that it would have got her if I had not held her.

That is nonsense. She would have to be unconscious and lying still for a longish time before the puma would have dared to investigate. I told her it was certainly a dog. I don't want her to catch the jitters from Mario and Teresa. If she is to be happy here, she must have absolute confidence that the llano is just as empty under the stars as under the sun.

Anyway she has never before set eyes on a puma — jaguar, yes. One cannot judge accurately the size of the big felines. I am told that they seem of immense length and impossible narrowness when they spring. Yet the same fellow rolled up asleep is just a furry ball and could easily be a dog, and not a very large one at that. I suspect that I saw what I wanted to see and that it was in fact a stray dog. Santa Eulalia crawls with them, all too bloated with beef offal to travel far from home. But the guerrilleros may well take along a few dogs for hunting. Alternatively it could have been put ashore to earn its own living by some Indian who was tired of its demands for a more dog-like diet than bananas.

[*April 3, Sunday*]

I like Chucha's smell — an undefinable blend of young animal and fresh vegetable. But I don't like my own. At dawn this morning I felt remarkably clean inside and filthy with stale sweat outside. So I got up, had a shower, climbed the wall so as not to wake up Mario by opening the gate and strolled out over the cool, gray llano.

For the first time I saw cattle between the creek and the forest. What is left of the grazing there seems to me exceptionally good, but beasts are never allowed to stray round the north end of the marshes and down into the corridor. If they do, the llaneros give them up as lost. They say it is because there is no intervening strip of parkland where the cattle could easily be rounded up. Certainly the forest is dense and begins abruptly. On my explorations of it I have found that after cutting a first passage through the green wall one has little further need of the machete and can even ride at a walk under the big timber. The llaneros may be right in holding that if a man tries to follow the cattle he merely drives them deeper into the forest and loses himself into the bargain. But they give up too easily. It's their distaste for the forest which counts.

As soon as the sun began to bite — which it does within twenty minutes of clearing the horizon — the cattle drifted into the shade and disappeared. To get on the wrong side of the creek they must have broken away from a bunch up north. It seems unlikely that they could not have been rounded up in the open. Was a small herd being driven towards the Cordillera through parkland unfamiliar to the llaneros?

I also searched for tracks of our visitor, but could find none — not surprising since the ground is as hard as a city pavement. Dead grass showed an impression where something had lain down about twenty yards from the house. I also found a dropping, but it looked more human than animal.

[*April 4, Monday*]

For civilized man — if I still am — it is a refreshing experience to be sexually and aesthetically satisfied, yet not emotionally involved. Love, no. Tenderness, yes. No concern for the future beyond a firm intention to preserve her as she is. No concern for her past except gratitude that it has led to so satisfactory a present.

I must admit that I am curious to know at what age she ceased to be Samuel's pet monkey and became his mistress. There does seem to have been a transition. But I lay off the subject, and with natural good taste she rarely mentions him. She is nearly as neat and hairless as an infant. Obviously she has never had a child. I suppose that problem is bound to crop up. I shouldn't be surprised if Joaquín has some earth-shaking remedies for it.

I find to my amazement that she can very slowly read. Samuel taught her. While I am working in the laboratory she respectfully ferrets about among books, papers and written scraps, watching me to see if all is permitted. Her curiosity is unceasing, and I try never to show impatience.

The patterns of mathematical formulas fascinated her.

[67]

"How do they tell a story, Ojen?" she insisted.

Ojen is the nearest she can get to Owen. With the help of a box of matches she easily grasped the principle of algebra. Either she has exceptional intelligence or I should make a very good father.

I should not like her to find Valera's letter. I doubt if she would understand its complexities, but no woman could miss the tone of contempt. So I have torn it up after translating it and have rewritten the diary entry of March 31 to include my English version of it.

I do not know whether she is happy, or merely ecstatic at so miraculous a change in her life. Perhaps the difference between the two can no more be analyzed for Chucha than for a child. I am disconcerted by her innocence. An odd word to use. I wrote it without thinking, but it's true. She has the innocence and goodness of the savage. Well, more the animal than the savage. The complicated mind of the savage is repulsive to anyone but an anthropologist. Chucha is all simplicity. I suppose that's what I mean.

Her religious beliefs are on a par with those of the llaneros. Jesus was kind and hangs on a cross in churches. God is very far away and of dubious importance. But the Virgin is all love and answers prayers. I gather that Chucha and Teresa are pooling their knowledge of the subject. It would be blasphemy to add any commentary of my own. I feel that those two and the Mother of God all understand each other very well.

[*April 6, Wednesday*]

I really must stop rogering Chucha afternoon and night and get on with my work. She is setting an example. She remembers nothing of the cereals and tubers of the altiplano but has picked up some knowledge of nursery gardening while trotting along behind mother in the plantations of the Montaña. With Mario's permission she has taken over the care and watering of his few peaches, lemons and oranges and is trying to raise a lime cutting in the shade. I just managed to prevent myself giving a lecture and telling her that she was doing it all wrong. But she must have green fingers. Not a leaf has flagged or dropped.

I shall give up this diary altogether. There is no need for it. I haven't the time in the evenings and I am no longer interested in fortifying myself against a blank spot which isn't there.

[*April 7, Thursday*]

No need for it? The devil must have been looking over my shoulder if he ever comes as far afield as the llanos of Colombia. Put it this way: I do not need a personal diary, but it looks as if I might need a record of facts. So, having got into the habit, I will keep it up.

This morning I thought Chucha was asleep, but she suddenly raised her head from the odd position where it had collapsed and said:

"Ojen, there is a horse coming."

I couldn't hear a thing myself. There was absolute silence. I have noticed that she seems to be able to hear sound waves through the ground as well as through air. They arrive, of course, much quicker.

As soon as I too heard it, I slipped on shirt and trousers and put a clip into the Lee-Enfield. I doubt if I should have bothered if I had been alone. It was papa being over protective. All the same, the incident was more than unusual. The rider had come from Santa Eulalia in the dark, which the llaneros will not, and he was traveling at a much faster pace than they ever do.

Mario had recognized the visitor and opened the gate by the time I got there. It was Pedro, riding his gray gelding bareback with only a halter. He had been using his spurs in good earnest. The beast was bleeding, fighting for breath and full of alarm.

He did not dismount and for once wasted no time in empty speech.

"They are going to cut my throat, friend! I have no hope but you."

He begged me to give him quickly as much food as he could carry and to ride with him to the edge of the forest. He had nothing at all with him but his machete and an old revolver tucked in his belt.

He was not a man to miss a chance of explaining himself dramatically and at length, so I knew that the affair was urgent and that he had good reason to be afraid. I told Mario to throw into a sack rice, dried and canned meat, matches and whatever he could lay his hands on instantly while I saddled up my reliable Estrellera. The disk of the sun was half above the horizon as we galloped across the creek. In another five minutes we were skirting the edge of the forest towards the only possible passage for a horse which I myself had cut. It would take a lot of finding for anyone who did not know it was there.

As soon as we were clear of the undergrowth and into the trees I dismounted and asked him what the devil was the matter.

He told me that four llaneros had been driving a small herd towards the foothills. Where they were going he, Pedro, did not know. But when they were two days out, nearing the rendezvous where the herd would be taken over, they had been machine-gunned from the air, the cattle scattered and two llaneros killed.

The other two, panicked by the discovery that aircraft could shoot, had ridden back to Santa Eulalia. A mere hour ago they had routed Pedro out of bed, told him to get dressed and firmly shut the door on his wife. They then said that they were going to cut his beautiful brown throat and that, as he had once been a friend, they would stretch it tight and do a neat job. He was a traitor who had sent them off on this errand and then told the government about it on his tac-tap machine.

To me Pedro protested that it was all a mistake and that, as I knew, he never mixed himself up in politics. To them he had said that they might as well have a last drink together — a proposal which appealed to the llaneros' curious sense of humor.

Keeping the bar counter between himself and the naked knives, he picked up a bottle and hurled it at the lantern which one of them was carrying. That of course set the store on fire. Pedro's rotgut was every bit as inflammable as spilled paraffin. In the confusion he yelled to his wife to get out, jumped on his horse and took off across the llano. How he came to have spurs on I can't imagine. I suppose they were always attached to his boots, though his normal pursuits were sedentary.

"They are close behind you?" I asked.

"Not very close. But now that it is day they will ride harder."

"How can they tell where you went?"

Not an intelligent question. It seemed to me that he could take off into space and not see another human being for days. But of course they knew that he had not even saddle and bridle. He would have to eat raw beef unless he lit a telltale fire. He dared not let his horse rest and graze unless he kept hold of the halter, for no South American horse — except rarities like my Tesoro — can easily be caught. Water he could only find at well-known points, giving his presence away by disturbing the cattle. The forest was his only hope, and the estancia his only source of supply.

His intention was to make his way southwest to the banks of the Guaviare and wait there until he could hail a passing canoe. The crossing of the forest would not take him more than two days or perhaps three, but he might have to wait much longer before seeing any movement on the river.

I asked him if he had a compass.

"Pedro needs no compass, friend. I am accustomed."

"Suppose they follow you?"

"Have you ever seen any of them between the estancia and the trees? No! Since they are determined to kill me, there will be several of them together. When they have given each other courage, they will ride along the edge of the forest but they will not enter it."

That was certain. They never went where they could not ride.

Thinking of the days of waiting on the riverbank, I wished I had provided him with hooks and a line. I asked him if he was likely to find game. Even an armadillo might just make the difference between hardship and starvation.

"Nobody knows for sure. But there must be hunting."

"Joaquín told me there are no Indians there."

"Joaquín is a fool. There are. But they stay in the deep forest and I shall never be far from the edge of the llano. It is said they are very small. The less reason to be afraid of them! Now go with God before the fools come galloping up to the estancia and frighten your girl! Take my horse and keep it till we meet again!"

"What should I tell them?"

"They will not hold it against you. Any of them would help a friend without asking questions. Say that you gave me food and know nothing!"

Well, I do not. I am quite certain that it was Pedro who organized the meat supply and fairly certain that he never informed the Government. The interception of the herd was probably due to some clever work by Valera and his colleagues.

I have little fear for Pedro. The forest, almost impenetrable where it meets the llano, soon becomes as open as, say, a ruined church in which the pillars are still upright but a lot of the roof has fallen on the floor. With luck he should be near the riverbank sometime tomorrow. Cutting his way through the last half mile will be long and arduous, and then he may emerge into one of those vile tangles where water, land and vegetation are indistinguishable; but with the river as low as it is a shore of sand or gravel can never be far off.

Lord knows where this story of pygmies comes from! I have never heard it before. Provided they have always kept to the shelter of the trees it is no more or less possible than traveler's tales of hundred-foot anacondas.

Leading his gray gelding, I cantered Estrellera back to the estancia and noticed at least three places where the creek was quite dry between shallow pools. Chucha and Mario seemed ridiculously anxious about me. I had hardly unsaddled and turned both horses into the corral when five of the Santa Eulalia toughs galloped up, loudly demanding entry. I received them as if they were the sixteenth-century caballeros whose manners and cruelty they have inherited, and they were compelled to respond with a due measure of courtesies before coming to the point.

I gave them my word that Pedro was not in the estancia. He had asked for food, which I had given, and then I had ridden with him to the forest and taken his horse. He had told me only that some gentlemen had tried to cut his throat and set fire to his store, but did not say why. Could they enlighten me?

"A private affair," one of them replied, showing no disapproval at all of my behavior. "I need tell you only that he has well deserved it."

I watched them through field glasses vaguely searching the frontier between trees and llano, and saw no more of them till they called in for a drink, two hours before sunset, on their way back to Santa Eulalia.

[*April 9, Saturday*]

I found Chucha crying this morning. She was comforting her lime sapling, or else it was comforting her. It is a totem, like a vegetable and living Teddy Bear, with which she takes refuge in trouble. She would not tell me what the matter was. I hope the loneliness is not getting on her nerves. She is a creature of closed horizons, of mountain valleys and rivers. This vast emptiness may oppress her. One needs to travel over it on a horse, not to look at it hopelessly from our oasis.

[75]

At first she was as frightened of the horses as her ancestors in Peru. For her they were alarming and self-willed animals with ferocious sets of teeth, only to be handled by the Conquerors and certainly not by humble women. Neither Tesoro nor Estrellera was helpful. Tesoro is only half broken by European standards — and Estrellera was very well aware that at last she had a human being in front of her who could be bullied.

But Chucha's ancestral inferiority complex is now on the way to be cured. Partly this is due to the presence of the llaneros the other evening. They were showing off in front of a pretty girl how magnificently they ride, yet they were all much darker skinned than she is. And partly it is due to Pedro's Pichón, who has gone out of his way to be polite to her ever since she nervously offered him the first carrot he had ever tasted. He likes women anyway. Pedro's wife used to treat him as a pet. He is a proper corporal's horse, quiet and unintelligent, willing to carry a pack or a rider. I think I can persuade Chucha to sit on his back.

But what can she wear? That's a problem which Teresa, who dresses in a single shapeless garment with one of my old shirts underneath, would be unable to solve. Nothing at all is the right answer. It would be less indecent than a skirt rucked up round her waist; but both Chucha and Teresa would certainly be shocked at the thought of an Indian Lady Godiva. I should also fear for the pale primrose skin on the inner part of her thighs. The *chiripá* of the Argentine pampas would look very well on her. I must try to remember how the length of cloth used to be folded and fixed in position.

[*April 10, Sunday*]

I made a dashing job of the *chiripá* by cutting up a green nylon pup tent which it is unlikely I shall ever want. The little darling thought the whole business of fitting the square around and between her legs most improper. In an obscure way I can understand the taboo. The business of a male is to undress, not to take a too intimate delight in dressing. Naturally enough I was entranced by this unexpected modesty. She responded, but still seemed disturbed. Enjoyment without joy. I must be more considerate and stop behaving like an archduke in a high-class brothel.

In the first cool of the evening I mounted her on Pichón — who fortunately approved of the *chiripá* — and suggested that we ride to the edge of the forest. She wouldn't hear of crossing the creek; so we walked our horses up the east side of the marshes where she became more cheerful and exclaimed at the colors of the birds. I should like to dress her in flamingo feathers. A vulgar thought! It offends against her simplicity. In any case I have to be content to set off her prettiness with things folded and belted like the *chiripá*. It would be reasonable to ask the Mission to fly in a sewing machine.

It has just occurred to me that Pedro's tac-tap is out

[77]

of action, so that it will take anything from three weeks to a month to make a request and get a reply. Well, we are remarkably self-sufficient.

[*April 11, Monday*]

This is the devil! I promised myself that nothing should hurt her while she was in my care, and now she is heading straight for tragedy.

There were tears again during the siesta; so I petted and encouraged her until the reason came out.

"Porque te quiero, Ojen."

I do not know how far the Indian of the altiplano shares our conception of love. Did the Conquerors import romantic love along with their music, speech and religion? I think I must assume they did, though all the evidence I have is that she looked straight into my eyes when she said she loved me and foresaw that there could be no happy ending.

I replied of course that I loved her too, but she knew very well that my *te quiero* did not mean the same as hers. What am I to do about this when the time comes? Love is a quite unnecessary serpent in our Eden. Valera would laugh and ask me what the hell I expected. Yet I didn't expect it. I could shrug my shoulders if Chucha had been a whore responding desperately to kindness and admiration. But what she feels and cries about is not, I think, that fairly predictable response. It is far nearer a child's unthinking, wholehearted love. I

[78]

can't reject it and I don't want to. There is a father/ daughter relationship between us. I cannot act as my own psychiatrist, but I suspect that if I had not been using her body with immense physical and aesthetic satisfaction I could have answered with absolute sincerity and in a quite different sense that I loved her. Am I suffering from the stupid contempt of the male for the woman he has bought? But I didn't buy her. She was a present.

I told her that I thought she had been crying because she was lonely. She replied that she could never be lonely any more because she would remember me even if I was not there. I wonder if she read that slowly in some ragged page torn from a magazine or if it came from the heart. Does it matter? Words must have a source. Then for no reason at all she suddenly saw the comic side of the *chiripá* and started to giggle. Her moods travel like the flickering of wind over the rushes.

"Now that we understand each other . . ." she began.

That, too, was spoken out of a child's instinct. There was a peace and confidence between us which, I see, I had hardly given a chance to grow.

"Now that we understand each other, promise me you will never go to the trees!"

I assumed that in some way she did not wish me to be associated with her past. I am always creating complexities where there aren't any.

I explained that it was my trade to go to the trees:

[79]

that anything which grew on the llano in partial shade was of interest to me and that we knew far too little of conditions of soil and geology at the border. That was beyond her. I put it more simply. Why does the forest stop where it does and not somewhere else?

"And I do not go at night," I added.

Nor I do. Like the llaneros, I have no exaggerated respect for predators, but it is obviously unwise to ride in the dusk where close cover overhangs the grass.

"Not in the day either," she insisted. "Never!"

This smelled of the blank spot again. She had talked to the llaneros only in my presence, so the bad influence had to be Mario.

"Listen, love! Mario has told me a dozen times what I must do and what I must not. Except in the matter of growing pimientos, I pay no attention."

"But he has not told you about the dwarfs."

I took this very seriously in order to get it all out of her. I pretended annoyance with Mario and demanded why he had not warned me.

"It is not right to speak of them."

I told her that they enjoyed being talked about, that Mario was trying to frighten little girls. There was a dwarf who rode on the necks of horses and plaited the manes. The llaneros and I not only spoke of him but cursed him to hell.

"Was Mario afraid that I would leave the estancia?"

"At first, yes. But not now. He says that if you believed they were there, you would go and talk to them."

What a compliment! To the scientific spirit of inquiry? Or to the essential humanity of Christian culture? But it left the main question of whether they were duendes or pygmies unsettled.

"What else did Mario say?"

"I told him about the dog. He said it belonged to them and that we must take good care when dogs can cross the creek. That is all."

Odder and odder. That a race of forest pygmies could exist is possible. Between the Cordillera and the llanos they would have more than thirty thousand square miles to play in — a primordial, uninteresting area the size of Scotland and just as unexplored as Scotland would be if travelers were confined to the Great Glen, the Forth and the Clyde.

Against their reality and in favor of myth or a folk memory is this nonsense of dogs. If they have dogs they must have been exposed at some time to Spanish influence. Then there would be some written record of them, perhaps two or three hundred years old. Even if lost, it would be alive as rumor and I should surely have heard it among a dozen other yarns of man-eating trees and Eldorados. I cannot believe that the memory should be entirely confined to Santa Eulalia.

I shall ride over tomorrow and see what I can extract from Joaquín.

[*April 12, Tuesday*]

Pedro's store is burned to the ground. No doubt the Government will give him some compensation when the news gets through, which could be several weeks unless Pedro himself quickly finds river transport. Meanwhile his poor wife is living wretchedly in an abandoned hut. She must in fact be far from destitute, but is naturally unwilling to dig up her flour bags from the ashes in the sight of all. Loyalty to Pedro. She must not lose the money which is to buy that tavern in Bogotá, however much she suffers meanwhile. I shall send some food, and I have told her that if she needs petty cash she can borrow from me. Marvelous generosity! She couldn't use more than about sixpence a day if she tried.

Joaquín was drying fish in the sun. They stink to high heaven and then become sweet. I find them quite edible if stewed like salt cod with plenty of garlic and tomatoes. So I bought a few from stock in order to vary our diet and encourage so exacting a craft.

"I have a question, Joaquín," I said at last, "for your wisdom in such matters is greater than mine. What should a man do if he meets a dwarf?"

He did not answer, busying himself with the fish, and finally spoke more to himself than to me.

"They will not cross water."

"Can they climb?"

"It is said they cannot."

[82]

That ruled out monkeys, which anyway are one of the staple foods of forest Indians and so familiar that they could not be feared. As for ground-living apes, it is certain that there are not and never were any in the Americas.

"Have you ever seen one?"

"Never. My father did."

"What did it look like?"

"Who knows what he has seen in the dusk?"

"They don't come out in the day?"

"All such things dread the sun."

"They are duendes?"

"It could be."

"What else is said about them?"

"They dance."

I let that go. Conversation with Joaquín has the advantage that neither party is necessarily expected to say anything for minutes on end. Whether he spends the intervals thinking or merely sitting I do not know. I myself find them useful for chewing over what he has said and working out the next move. This time I had an inspiration worthy of an anthropologist.

"Is that why there was no guitar in Santa Eulalia?"

"That is why."

"But have the dwarfs ever come so far to dance?"

"Who knows?"

"And at the estancia?"

"It is said that Manuel Cisneros saw them."

"Have you ever heard that they hunt with dogs?"

[83]

"What need would they have of dogs?"

That was all I could get out of him. For Pedro they were real and neither more nor less to be feared than any other unapproachable tribe. For Joaquín they are clearly duendes.

Yet his treatment of the subject differed from the matter-of-fact way in which he usually describes the various spirits which surround us. The llaneros too seem to feel a distinction. They believe, of course, in duendes but will not normally allow them to interfere with their daily life. The dwarfs do interfere. They are responsible for the llaneros' reluctance to travel at night between Santa Eulalia and the estancia, and also for the fact that the grazing west of the marshes and the creek is never used.

I wish Tesoro could speak. There may be some scent from the forest or some trick of the light which alarms horses. That would be enough to create a legend and to cause the abandonment of the estancia through lack of labor. If one's only method of transport proves unreliable without any explanation, one falls back on gremlins like aircraft pilots in the last war. A pity that I cannot materialize some arms and legs on these forest fairies and put them to work on irrigation channels!

[*April 13, Wednesday*]

I have tackled Mario and laid down the law that he is not to frighten Chucha with a lot of nonsense. I got

[84]

little of interest out of him except confirmation that dwarfs don't climb. That is why he is always mending walls and stopping up holes which a little chap could squeeze through.

He admitted that low morale was the reason for the estancia being deserted. Cattle grazing in the corridor between creek and forest had been lost. In the llano beyond the marshes, where the line of the trees sweeps away to the northwest, horses had vanished into the darkness and once a man. Why not, I asked, an increase in the number of jaguars following a favorable year for the game? No, the llaneros ruled out jaguars. But why in God's name dwarfs? Because they had been seen dancing. How far away and how much light? Close to the estancia and dark. Any moon? Don't know.

It was all worthless evidence, with a slight bias in favor of actual, physical hunters from the forest. On a starlit night one's eyes pick up movement at, say, seventy yards, and can vaguely recognize size and gait. That is to say, I could not distinguish with certainty a cow from a horse or a puma from a big dog, but I could distinguish a man from any of them.

"So the llaneros killed Manuel Cisneros," I said in the hope that he would be surprised into confessing it. I could then be sure that they had made up the whole story.

"No, Don Ojen, no! He went away when he could get no one to herd the cattle."

"Why didn't you go too?"

[85]

"What should I do? I am not a llanero. We must eat, Teresa and I and the boys who were then at her skirts. And he gave me the paper saying that I might stay as long as I liked."

"But all the time you were afraid?"

"Not much. In the day, as you know, what could be more peaceful? At night one must stay indoors. Then there is no danger."

"How do you know there isn't?"

"Because there never has been."

Not a satisfying answer on the face of it. But knowledge can only be founded on experience. How do I know there isn't a blue orange? Because there never has been.

My summing up has to be — with a mass of reservations — in favor of pygmies. Here is a picture of them:

1. They are hunters and food-gatherers like the most primitive of the forest Indians. They only leave the shelter of the trees after sunset or before sunrise. Sound enough. That is when the deer, peccary and small game are to be found browsing at the edge of the llano.

2. They will come as far as the estancia in rare and exceptional years when the creek can be crossed.

3. They won't wade (? fear of alligators or eel) and they clearly have no canoes or their presence would have been reported on the river. This is hard to believe. They must have seen canoes and their culture cannot be so primitive that they are unable to build one.

4. They are very timid and won't face a wall. Won't,

I think, not can't. Presumably they have observed this place for years and know that it is inhabited by very large men on very strange animals.

5. Tribal dances take place at night on the llano. A forest glade seems a more natural choice; but one must not underrate the power of religious tradition. Perhaps they lived in the open some thousands of years ago.

Having put this down on paper, I feel it adds up to beings as improbable as duendes. You pays your money and you takes your choice. But I am determined to know. To be the discoverer of Homo Dawnayensis really would be something!

[*April 15, Friday*]

Teresa tells me that we are shortly going to run out of coffee. That is where Pedro's store was useful. He could always keep us going with staples if I forgot to order in time or the Government Canoe failed to deliver. One would expect some inquiries about him, but it is not surprising that the Intendencia shows no curiosity. I doubt if Pedro transmitted a message a month before I came here. He sent off his reports and did his ordering by the canoe.

Perhaps it is my duty to let somebody know what has happened, since I am the only citizen for miles around who can write. But what with pygmies, fornication and fatherliness I have hardly given a thought to Pedro. I don't know the movements of the Government

[87]

Canoe — Pedro was the only person who could make a reasonable guess — and I refuse to spend days in Santa Eulalia waiting for the chance to send off a letter. Mañana! One of these days the Intendencia or the Mission will send somebody to see how I am getting on.

We may have had a visit. I woke up at five to hear Tesoro neighing, and some plunging in the corral. So I went out, suspecting that my pair of beauties might have set about Pichón. They do not see why he should have carrots while they get stale bread. Answer: carrots are too precious to be used for wholesale bribery.

I found all the horses sweating. Tesoro had stamped an agouti into the dust. Was the agouti responsible for the excitement, or was there anything else which panicked the horses? My only reason for suspecting there might be is the improbability of an agouti entering our compound at all and then taking refuge in the corral. Mario of course showed no sign of life. He hears nothing and sees nothing, safe from duendes and disturbances behind his closed doors.

I searched the llano with my torch from various points of vantage but saw nothing. When I returned to the house I threw open the shutters on the south side to see if the first gray of morning showed any movements between estancia and forest. It did not. One might as well be out to sea in an absolute calm.

[*April 16, Saturday*]

On the other shore of that sea are a bunch of frightened and murderous outlaws. Should I have foreseen what was on the way to me? I prefer duendes with no politics to men with them.

This afternoon the Cuban and two other fellows, all bristling with automatic weapons, arrived in a jeep — the first motor vehicle I have ever seen in this vast corner of the llanos. They put a lot of trust in their weatherman. If the rains caught them in the middle of nowhere, they would have to get back to the Cordillera on foot.

In Santa Eulalia they had found nobody to bully except women and children who did not even understand their questions. Futility and the searing heat had not improved their tempers. Chucha took one look at the party and dashed into the kitchen where she deliberately dirtied her face and hair to give the impression of some sort of half-witted slut working for her food. She instinctively felt that these three sullen revolutionaries had appeared from a traditionless world and might not even have the dubious, vestigial chivalry of the llaneros.

I received them as caballeros, for which they did not give a damn. Marxism is too mannerless a creed for Latin America.

The Cuban wanted to know if Pedro had been killed or not. He had no evidence one way or the other but a pile of ashes. I said that I had every reason to believe

[89]

Pedro was alive, failing very bad luck, and explained what he had told me and how he had escaped.

"He was much too frightened of you to give your plans away," I added.

"How do you know he was?"

"Because any fool could read his thoughts. He never could keep his mouth shut."

"So it was you who informed the Government?"

I replied that I knew no details. Even if I had, how could I have passed them on?

"There are aircraft which come down here."

"Not since your last visit."

"You expect me to believe that?"

"Go back to Santa Eulalia tonight and ask. At least one horseman would have seen the plane and by the time it comes down there are always two or three of them on the spot, like ants."

"Have your servants in!"

He could not let them off without a homily. Mario, Teresa and Chucha were lectured on the joys of a society in which ruthless capitalists would no longer own the land and exploit their labor. I did not point out that Mario was the only landowner present.

Mario was quite calm and unaffected. He said that not a soul had visited the estancia but Pedro and the llaneros who were after him.

"When did your master last go to Santa Eulalia?"

"On Tuesday."

"And before that?"

Mario genuinely could not remember. Owing to anxiety over the lack of water and then the arrival of Chucha, I had not been in Santa Eulalia since the guitar-playing evening. He said that the last time the Government Canoe called he had gone himself to meet it.

"What for?"

I was relieved that Mario offered no unnecessary information. He just said that he had gone to fetch our stores.

"Did you send off any letters?"

"Yes, many."

I interrupted to point out that it was unlikely any of them could have reached Bogotá yet. I was poked in the belly with a machine pistol and told to shut up.

Teresa came next. Since she never left the estancia, she merely confirmed what Mario had said. If he had claimed to have visited the sun, she would have backed him up. The Cuban disregarded her mumblings and tried Chucha.

"Where do you come from?"

"I am Peruvian."

"And what do you do here?"

"I am a servant."

"Do you sleep with the master?"

"Of course."

"Why of course?"

"Because I like to."

This reply was too simple for the Cuban. I translated his snort of disapproval to mean that any little Indian would feel affection for any capitalist lecher who was kind to her.

"How did you get here?"

"By the Canoe."

"Who paid your passage?"

"Captain Valera," she answered proudly.

She thought all these chaps with guns must belong to the same incomprehensible, ungentle society and that Valera's name would command respect. Her entire conception of politics is that one should avoid policemen. They shut you in gaol until you consent to pull your skirts up.

The Cuban dismissed them all to the kitchen and started to undo his pistol holster. I was not impressed — or managed to persuade myself that I was not. The fellow was irresponsible, but presumably part of a chain of command. I thought it wise to remind him of it.

"I admit that Valera is a friend of mine," I said. "But so, I hope, is the gentleman who accompanied you on your last visit."

"You knew what was planned."

"I guessed it and told you so frankly, but I could not know time and place. A little logic, friend! Pedro said nothing, but let us assume he did. Then what is the only way I could pass the information on? Through Pedro! So why bring me in at all?"

"It would do me good to shoot you," he said.

I replied that it was quite safe to shoot me, that my

servants would run away and my body would not be found for weeks. He should not be selfish, however. Someone else might like to interrogate me and have the pleasure of shooting me afterwards.

"I shall report to my headquarters," he said, "and then come back to fetch you."

To that I could only answer that I should be delighted to see him at any time, and would he and his party like a few vegetables for their journey?

To my astonishment he accepted them, saying that I was very different from other Anglo-Saxons.

"On the contrary, I am a typical Anglo-Saxon," I said. "The Americans are not. They are no more Anglo-Saxon than Filipinos are Spanish. A revolutionary should not confound national origins with language."

When they had driven away I was left gasping at myself. Insolence combined with extreme courtesy is just the sort of quality which in the French Revolution would have sent an aristocrat to the guillotine next morning. But I am neither aristocrat, landowner or capitalist, and my courtesy is only a flower upon the normal, upcountry manners of Argentina. It makes them stop and scratch their heads. Also it emphasizes the superiority of the classless scientist, and that is what they want to believe. Marching together under the Workers' Flag we shall reform society. Balls from the Thoughts of Mao, or vice versa. I shall go and give Chucha a bath.

[*April 18, Monday*]

I am fully occupied by Chucha who wants to be taught to ride and to write. Writing is just a matter of practice. She recognizes the letters and their phonetic values, but cannot imitate them. I can find an exact parallel from personal experience. I know the difference between Estrellera's forearm and Tesoro's, but I'm damned if I can draw it.

Samuel's system of primary education was to teach her words or syllables, not individual letters. The reason seems to have been that they had a couple of books — half a *Don Quixote* and a handbook of butterflies — but seldom any paper. I do not wish to discuss Samuel more than I must. I salute him from a distance. One of his sources of income was the capture and mounting of butterflies. But Chucha, to his credit, was not for sale.

I am getting her used to Pichón before we start on the elementary aids. Today I took her over the creek, up the west side of the marshes and then across to the forest at a gentle canter. She was so occupied by staying on — or rather by her own pride in staying on without difficulty — that we were only half a mile from the trees before she realized it and squeaked.

I dismounted at once in the shade of a palm — partly because I had already decoyed her nearer to the forest than I thought possible, partly because her blowing hair and the green *chiripá* were sending me crazy. When I lifted her down from Pichón, I found that she

[94]

was just as impatient. After that first mutual explosion
I took the sheepskin off Tesoro and made her more
comfortable while the horses grazed.

It was a good moment to reinforce her growing confidence. I asked her as she lay in my arms why she was
so afraid of Mario's ridiculous duendes.

"I am not afraid of anything with you," she said.

She is not. I wonder what her mental picture of me
really is. That remark from a civilized woman would
mean nothing. A charming, trivial erotic response. But
Chucha means it as sincerely as a child of five. I am
number two to God. Fortunately I cannot disillusion
her. I write "fortunately" because I do not know
whether I should or I shouldn't.

When we had remounted I took her at her word, and
we rode back along the forest: a motionless face of bril-
liant, light green until the sun disappeared behind the
cloud of the treetops and the continual death of plants
became as obvious as the abounding life. It was the
same forest that she knew and no more remarkable
when seen from a horse than from her rivers. Monotony after monotony, and always safe so long as a man
can carry his food and find enough water.

She promised that she would not worry so long as I
took Tesoro with me on my explorations of the botanical frontier. It is curious that she should realize his
watchdog qualities when she does not yet recognize exactly how he shows anxiety. He was on edge all the time
and fighting my hands, but I was able to pass off his

nervousness as greed. I said that he wanted to go closer and see what was edible among such a luscious variety of green stuff. In fact he was set on bolting for the brown llano. He strongly dislikes the forest and is inclined to shy at nothing — which makes him as poor a guardian as a watchdog which barks at everything.

This evening's ride has cleared the way. I have two objects in wanting to spend whole days in the forest. One is to see if there is any evidence at all of the little hunters. Since I have little woodcraft, it would have to be obvious enough for any boy scout — the ashes of a fire, an arrowhead, a blazed tree, something of that sort. The other object is to find a place of refuge for Chucha and myself. I am confident that I can deal with any ordinary bandit and talk him out of unnecessary violence; but political idealists on the run are new to me. It is possible that this obstinate Cuban might return to the estancia with orders to snatch me up to the Cordillera or shut my mouth for good. In that case — assuming I could reach the horses — I should have to try Pedro's trick and find safety for us both in the forest.

[*April 19, Tuesday*]

I must make this a long and exact entry: a record of facts to which I may someday have to refer in public. What public? There is no public. I wish Valera would return or that a plane would come in out of the blue or that some wireless operator would notice that there are never any messages from Pedro. I am here to conduct experiments in tropical agriculture. I am not the secret agent of the CIA or any other bunch of prejudiced whore-cum-spymasters. And I am not to be lied to and double-crossed by a damned mulatto murderer who happens to have read a handbook on the interrogation of suspects — if he can read.

At dawn I saddled Tesoro, who could carry me farther into the forest than I had penetrated by any of my cursory explorations on foot. I knew that, once in the tall timber, the trunks were far enough apart for man and horse, provided always that the rider was not aiming for any particular point and was content to go where he could.

My excuse to Chucha was hunting. We are short of fresh meat. So I took the Lee-Enfield on the off chance of meeting deer or peccary. I also took a small bundle of colored beads, iron nails and dried fish wrapped in a length of the bright green pup tent. I felt slightly absurd playing at Robinson Crusoe, but it seemed the best method. If I laid out a present in some prominent place and it subsequently disappeared, I could rule out duendes.

I would far rather have taken the mare but, since Chucha found some special magic in Tesoro, I had to ride him. He began to play up as soon as we had crossed the creek and had to be shown who was boss. The cut passage, through which I had taken Pedro, was already closed by fern and offshoots from the fallen scrub. I had to use the machete and lead Tesoro with the other hand. After that we had leaf mold under foot and could move generally westwards though never in a straight line. Silence was absolute, proving that two hundred feet above my head the sun was blazing on treetops and already inhibiting all activity. At dawn and in the cool of the evening I have known the forest as noisy as an ill-organized public meeting.

I was riding more or less parallel to the Guaviare, never turning towards it since the only certain thing about Homo Dawnayensis was that he had never been seen on the banks. Conditions were surprisingly favorable for game, though I saw none. I passed through two glades with good grazing, the first small and entirely open, like a green well in the surrounding forest; the second fairly open, without definite boundaries and gently sloping upwards towards the west. In both I expected to find that game had fed, but there were no droppings except a pat of cow dung — almost certainly from the lost beasts which I had seen on April 3 and now knew to be stragglers from the guerrilla's herd.

I rode at a good pace up the second glade until I was stopped by a low, overgrown cliff. That was what, sooner or later, I expected to see, for the stretch of grass and parkland could only mean that there was not enough soil for tree roots. When I had followed the outcrop of rock for half a mile to the north, it disappeared and the canopy of the forest closed overhead — big timber through which I could easily continue a westerly course.

Here and there to my left I could catch a glimpse of rising ground and thick vegetation, showing that I was traveling along the side of a low ridge where trees were confined to pockets and cracks in the rock, leaving enough light for secondary growth of shrubs. The place was uncannily silent except for Tesoro's hooves. The only sound I heard was unfamiliar — something between a whistle and a sea gull's call. It seemed to come from far away on the other side of the ridge; but among trees it is difficult — for me, at any rate — to tell whether a sound is weak and close or distant and strong. This, I thought, had too much power behind it for a bird. A primitive, man-made instrument?

Soon I could see a confused mass of rocks above me, with gray pinnacles rising out of the jungle which crept and climbed over the lower stuff. These crags looked high enough to give me a view across the treetops — a rare experience of ethereal beauty. The dark green flows on as solidly as a garden, and eyes insist that one could walk from every dome of blazing flowers to another.

Since Tesoro could easily have broken a leg I tethered him to a tree and left him plunging and protesting. The ridge was a tangle of fallen, rotting trees, of roots, ravines and hollows. Patches of blue sky, red and orange macaws sailing in it with the ease of hawks, tempted me on, but I did not like it at all. Anything — especially

[99]

snakes — might be living in the dark holes where one could hardly distinguish plant from mineral. I unslung my rifle, which left me only one hand to climb with — and that got fiercely bitten by ants. However, they seemed to be the only inhabitants.

The top was just too low to allow me my view over the trees, but was open, desolate and no doubt a landmark which could be glimpsed from many points in the forest. Facing east was a great sloping slab of rock which I should probably have seen if I had climbed the low cliff at the upper end of the glade. I stripped off moss and cleared the cracks, leaving a whitish patch the size of a billiard table. There I laid out and firmly anchored my square of green nylon, spreading the presents on it. The patch of color could, of course, attract monkeys who would scatter the lot; but I had neither heard nor seen any monkeys since entering the forest when a band out on an egg-stealing expedition was raising hell among the birds.

The whole place was singularly lifeless, with not even a lizard. The only animal material at all was the point of an antler which I found when scraping earth from the slab. It was worn very smooth. Polished by man? Weatherworn? Or passed through the stomach of scavenger or jaguar?

I am used to desolation and normally excited by it, but there on the rocks I was not. That low plateau was somehow menacing. I felt that I was watched. Any of Joaquín's duendes could have had it all his own way if he had stuck up his sabre-toothed head from a hole or hidden behind a pinnacle. I do not think that human beings would choose to live in such a tangle of primeval litter when there is shelter on the forest floor, less risk of basking snakes and less annoyance of ants. All the same I have to return to explore further and to see what, if anything, I have attracted. The ridge continues to the southwest, and must be the only landmark between the llano and the Guaviare.

It was now after two and time to turn back. By following the contours I found the head of the long glade without difficulty, and was able to make for the smaller, well-like glade on a compass course. There I allowed Tesoro to graze a little — though he seemed more interested in staying close to me — while I searched on foot for the gap we must have made on our outward journey. I could not find it. We had pushed through giant ferns for the last few yards and the fronds had sprung back into position.

However, it did not matter where we left the glade; so when I spotted a break on the southern side — more a marked difference of foliage than a gap — I decided to try it. A fallen tree had brought the lianas down with it, and a palisade of saplings was growing through the debris. I knew that this mess was not as formidable as it looked, that it would not continue far and that I could easily cut a passage through which to lead Tesoro back into the darkness of the trees.

Once across the fallen trunk I saw to my right the

clean cut stalk of a cedar sapling and then a dozen other neat cuts which could only have been made by a machete in experienced hands. It was a thousand to one that I was on the track of Pedro. No one else could have been there so recently.

For a moment I could not believe in the coincidence, but then I saw that there wasn't any. He had entered the forest where I had, and both of us had then taken the easiest route, always going round obstructions rather than over or through them — he, because he wanted to put distance quickly between himself and the llaneros; I, because I wanted to ride as far as possible in a day without much caring where. He had observed the change of vegetation which promised sunlight and more open country and somewhere had forced his way into the glade, no doubt hoping that he was going to find parkland as far as the Guaviare.

When he was at last in the well of grass, he had looked for a possible path to the south and had seen, just as I had, the hopeful break. He cut his way out on a more professional track, round the upturned roots of the tree, so I missed the marks of his machete altogether — visibility being down to about four feet — until I was over the tree and nearly out.

The temptation to see how truly he had headed south ("Pedro needs no compass") was overwhelming, although there could be no trace of his passage until I came to some other barrier. I doubt if even an Indian could discover very much from the forest floor itself.

However, I had time in hand and no fear of losing myself. I had only to turn east to arrive at the dividing wall of forest and llano.

There could be little doubt of Pedro's choice of a route once he was clear of the glade. An aisle as straight as that of a cathedral ran southwest for more than three hundred yards until it dissolved into randomly placed trunks. Crossing the end of it, I found a slight suggestion of a narrow path. Since the prevailing gloom of the forest showed no light and shade I could not tell for certain where the leaves had been beaten down and where they had not.

I may have imagined it. If the path existed, it ran fairly straight between the unexplored south side of the ridge and the llano. There were no slots of deer, peccary or tapir and no hoof marks; so bare feet were an attractive possibility. Pedro would have recognized at once whether or not it was a game trail, but would not as yet have gone out of his way to hunt. He was intent on the river, or so I thought, and the going in front of him was open and easy.

I came upon his body at the foot of a tree some distance to my left. The gleam of white caught my eye and I rode towards it, believing it to be a growth of fungus or epiphytes or possibly Loranthaceae. Bits of his clothing lay about on the ground, and the bones had been stripped clean of flesh by black ants which were still at work on it. He was holding his old revolver. An eerie sight it looked when grasped in a skeleton hand. The cause of death was immediately apparent. He had been shot twice at the base of the skull.

I broke open his gun. One round had gone off and the next had misfired. Dwarfs and llaneros were at once eliminated. The former had presumably no firearms; the latter, if they had followed up and killed Pedro, would have boasted about it on their return to the estancia. This was plainly a deliberate execution by the guerrillas. Since they could not have found him once he was in the forest, both he and the Cuban had lied to me. When I left Pedro at the cut passage he had been not only escaping from the llaneros but bound for a definite rendezvous. I should have suspected that he was not telling all the truth. I was too innocent.

The more I think of his murder, the angrier I am. I am too familiar with Latin America to be horrified by an armed struggle for political power. If men are willing to risk their lives, the strength of discontent is shown more accurately than by the public opinion polls which corrupt and distort our democracies. But cold-blooded execution of a harmless, babbling ex-corporal is another matter. It disgusts me that any human being should be so sure that he has a right to kill.

I examined Pedro's body as closely as I could without disarticulating the bones. No doubt it would have told some sort of story to an expert in forensic medicine; but I could deduce very little from the two bullet holes at the base of the skull, one on each side of the foramen magnum. One could guess at a small-calibre weapon. The absence of any severe shattering of the bone was proof that it had been fired at some little distance, probably when Pedro saw a chance to run and took it.

I had the impression that the body, lying in an awkward position with the head slumped against a tree root and both arms flung out, had been left exactly where it fell. In that case the actual bullets ought to be in the skull or on the ground, for there was no exit wound. I could not find them. It was not surprising. The soil around the skeleton had been disturbed by kites and lizards feeding on the flesh. None of the larger carnivores had found the body and cracked the bones, which suggested that there were few of them about.

I had nothing to bury him with, and it was of course impossible to carry back the dry bones on Tesoro. So I had to turn away and leave him under the protection of the little cross which he carried on a thin gold chain round his neck. I blazed trees at intervals on the random route I took back to the llano and made notes of compass bearings wherever obstructions compelled me to diverge from an easterly course. I could not record distances accurately, but I think I shall be able to lead an official inquirer — if there ever is one — to the body.

I hit the llano some two or three miles south of my point of entry and had no exceptional difficulty in getting myself and Tesoro out to the light. Till it was close on sunset I worked away with the machete, cutting and widening a new passage which should be easily recognizable even after a month.

At the estancia all was quiet and there was a rich smell of stew. Chucha admitted that she and Mario had been anxious until they saw me crossing the creek with no shadows following. I told them that nothing could be emptier than this last, lost tail end of the forests of the Amazon Basin — no game, no dwarfs and no duendes.

I did not mention Pedro, for fear of starting up the oppression of the blank spot. I should have had Mario building walls as fast as a Roman infantryman and Chucha putting on a face like the Mater Dolorosa every time I visited the trees. Teresa is the only matter-of-fact one of the lot. She assumes that my learning is so profound and mysterious that I must know what I am doing.

I wish I did know. I have a strong presentiment that I ought to take the three horses and Chucha and cross the llanos to the River Vichada. But I cannot leave Mario and Teresa without some protection — if only pseudo-aristocratic insolence — against these brutes of guerrilleros. They might come back and cut the throats of the family as pointlessly as they blew Pedro's brains out.

What a curious thing presentiment is! I felt no fear whatever, only pity and anger, when I found Pedro's body, although in the gloom of the trees it should have had the crude effect of some dangling oddment in a ghost train. Yet on the rocky plateau, where there was sunlight and not a damn thing to be afraid of, it was an effort to control imagination. In both cases Tesoro's reaction was the same as my own.

[*April 20, Wednesday*]

Today I rode to Santa Eulalia to buy beef. It is not always easy to find unless some llanero has driven home a beast on the previous night for local consumption. The only refrigerator for many hundreds of miles is mine, and meat will not keep in this climate. It is well hung — to say the least — by the time I unload it at the estancia.

I was lucky and got the sirloin and ribs of a heifer. But what a waste! I shall have to throw half of it away, for my refrigerator is small. Those pygmies could have meat for the asking if only there were some way of communicating with them.

I did nothing about Pedro's wife. God knows if I am right! I have two reasons for allowing her to go on hoping. I feel that the body should not be disturbed until someone in an official position turns up to view it. And if I say that I found him murdered I shall start a flaming argument among the llaneros, very likely to make another widow.

Perhaps my real objection is cowardly and selfish. Since nothing would induce the valiants of Santa Eulalia to fetch that body out of the forest — they dread touching the defunct anyway — I should have to do it myself. I don't mind tumbling poor Pedro into a sack, but my life and work could then become complicated if the National Liberation Army suspected that I had killed him and all the llaneros were convinced that the duendes did.

I called on Joaquín and showed him the antler point which I had picked up, asking him if it was any sort of Indian artifact. He was certain that it was not. He thought it might have worked its way out through the skin of boa or anaconda and been smoothed by the digestive juices.

"Do you think Pedro has reached the Guaviare?" I asked.

"No."

"What could have stopped him?"

"You know very well."

"What sort of weapons do they have?"

"None. What meets them dies of fright."

"Animals, too?"

"Yes."

I maintained the long silence demanded by Indian manners. I suppose it is not polite to make anyone think. Therefore speech should be confined to essentials. The European believes the opposite. He babbles to conceal the absence of thought.

"Neither you nor I have ever picked up an animal which died of fright," I said.

"If it is eaten, how do we know whether it dies of fright or arrow or bullet or claws or teeth?"

He almost chanted this as if it were the beginning of an epic.

"Did Pedro die of fright?"

"No. He was a brave man. But it is no use to shoot."

Since Joaquín was inexplicably sure of Pedro's death, I tested him a bit further.

"How many times did he shoot?"

"Once," he replied with utter, calm certainty. "Once only."

I didn't go into that. His explanations, when he can be persuaded to give any, are not intelligible.

"If I were killed," I asked, "would you see who did it?"

"No. But it could be I should hear you."

Some kind of rapport between Joaquín and any of his close friends in their moment of agony seems to me conceivable. It is odd that I should accept this more readily than the obvious solution: that the guerrilleros told, say, some woman who in turn told Joaquín.

I just don't believe it. The news would be all over Santa Eulalia. Pedro's wife would have received a formal visit of condolence and somebody, hand on heart, would have loosed off some antique oratory. Joaquín's character must also be considered. Though his mind is a ragbag of superstitions and absurdities — some of them not to be dismissed out of hand — he never makes mystery where there is none.

Certainly Pedro was the most unlikely person to die of fright. It is possible among animals. I have seen a rabbit chased by a stoat until it cowered in terror, incapable of movement. That or something like it is as near as a living creature can get to dying of fright from a natural cause.

I leave out the supernatural. I think one must admit that men have died of fright (shock? hypothermia?) because of something they saw. But that begs the question: what is seeing? The eye is only a camera; the picture has to be interpreted by the brain. When the brain has no experience of the object photographed, it interprets the message of the eye as it pleases. So what you think you are recording has far more relation to your beliefs than to the facts. That goes for politicians and policemen on one plane, and for Joaquíns on the other. It rarely goes for Pedros.

So home to find Chucha menstruating, damn it! She is far more sensitive on the point than civilized women. One would think that the closer a girl is to nature, the more she would understand that this is the period when she most urgently requires the male. But Chucha's propriety is positively Victorian. Gentlemen do not ask questions. Gentlemen do not kiss whatever may be available. And above all gentlemen do not cuddle and comfort in case the unspeakable should happen. What a lot of nonsense — the most universal and powerful taboo without a single fact to support it!

What astonishes me is that she isn't pregnant. I

know that I myself am not sterile, for there is a bitter memory of a doctor's bill which had to be paid in cash when I could least afford it. The sudden change of environment and diet might have affected Chucha's ovulation like that of an animal which cannot breed in captivity.

But how day by day I begin to admire the child! She is not in the least the submissive little person of three weeks ago. She is a proud person. Has love done that for her or have I? The first, of course. I never set out to make a companion of her or suspected that her adolescent, eager intelligence could become as irresistible as her body. I wonder if a gentleman would be permitted to say good night provided he made it sufficiently fatherly.

[*April 21, Thursday*]

In the doghouse. All my fault. Not even writing lessons permitted, let alone any other kind. I endeavor to meet Teresa's eyes with an expression of absolute innocence.

[*April 23, Saturday*]

Again an entry which is put down as a vital record of fact, omitting all Thoughts of Mao and self-analysis. It has all turned out better than I dared hope, though if the Colombian had not come along I doubt whether I should be here now.

When I saw the jeep bouncing down from the north over the llano I loaded my rifle and the 16-bore and hid them under the fodder alongside the corral. I knew that in the house I had not a hope of defending myself but if Chucha and I were ever given a chance to run for the horses I might be able to hold off pursuit.

There were three of them — the boss, a driver and that detestable tough I called the Cuban. In fact he turns out to be a Dominican. Why is it that these fearless fellows who dare to resist a dictator cannot resist his methods? Three were quite enough to deal with us. Besides their personal weapons they had a light machine gun mounted on the jeep.

It was close on sunset when they arrived, so I had to feed them and put them up for the night. I was reasonably polite but cold. If I had been certain that they intended to liquidate me I should probably have been greasily companionable in the hope of arousing some sympathy.

This time I insisted that Chucha should receive my so-called friends. She put on the white outfit in which she had arrived — with a shirt of mine underneath — and took the head of the table. I would not even have her hanging around in the provincial manner and serving the men while they ate. If the Dominican had come alone, I should never have risked this display of my pride in her, knowing that after my death she would be raped and abandoned. But the Colombian was a man of taste — so far as his political creed allowed — and I felt sure that he would take her along to the Cordillera where at least she would belong to him or one of his more decent officers. That was better than dying of disease or starvation in or out of a brothel.

She was too embarrassed to do any talking, but I think she found a secret pleasure in the compliments of the Colombian who gallantly took his cue from me and treated her as the daughter of the house. The driver, a pure Indian, could not take his eyes off her. That also made her feel a bit of a native princess. The situation could easily have fallen into ironic comedy. That it never did was due to her simplicity and her unaffected use of my Christian name.

After our supper I kissed her hand and told her to go to bed. She was quite delightful, giving a little bow to each of the guests. Even the Dominican had to smile and bow back.

"I see that Captain Valera was indeed a friend," the Colombian said.

"It is a pity that I have not yet been able to say thank you to him."

He got the point. So did his Number Two about twenty seconds later.

"You must understand, Doctor, that we are always in danger of our lives," he said. "We think they matter not only to us but to all America."

I replied that I did understand, but that it was no reason for interrogating me as if I were a spy for the Government or the Yankees and accusing me of being responsible for Pedro's death when they both knew very well that Pedro had been executed.

"He is dead?"

"When men are shot in the back of the head they usually are."

"Will you believe me when I swear that I know nothing of this?"

"I am not accustomed to doubt a man's word when he is armed and I am not."

"I wish you would not carry on like someone out of the last century," he said. "It must be the influence of the llaneros. None of my friends shot Pedro. I am telling you so. Where is his body?"

"In the forest."

"Can we go there in the morning?"

"Not in the jeep. But I can mount you both."

"Then there is no need for more discussion at present. One other demand, and afterwards I trust we can just be guests of a generous host. May we see your generator?"

"It's about enough to keep the beer cold and your beef from going rotten," I told him, "plus six electric bulbs."

I showed my neat little twelve-volt generator. He seemed satisfied that it could not be used for a radio transmitter — and probably saw as well that I had no notion whether it could or not. Thereafter our relations were much less formal, but I was far from sure of the Dominican thug.

I told Mario and Chucha that I should leave at dawn

for the forest with my friends. Mario did not question my description of them. He was used to the violent quarrels in Santa Eulalia, after which the participants became quite amicable. He showed none of his usual distrust of the forest. He must have reckoned that the three of us together could shoot the teeth out of any number of dwarfs.

The two guerrilleros stood by casually while I lifted fodder to give the horses a bite before starting. I observed with pleasure a tightening of their faces when I picked up my rifle with the muzzle on a level with their bellies. They hadn't a chance of drawing their pistols in time and their driver was far away under the jeep. I pretended to notice nothing and they relaxed.

As soon as we had ridden through my new passage I could see that neither of them had ever before traveled in the forests of the Amazon and Orinoco basins. They only knew the steaming slopes beneath the Cordillera where cliffs, ravines and all the rampant growth make it impossible to leave the track. You can't cut a way up and you can't fall down, and if you stand still long enough you can nearly watch the stuff growing over you.

The monotonous ride through the gloom, where only at intervals did we have to dismount and lead our horses, disturbed them. Life in the treetops was just dying down when we left the llano behind. Then came the silence, broken only by an occasional shriek. The Dominican wanted to know whether birds or monkeys were responsible. Neither, I said shortly, and shut up. It was of course a bird.

I did not draw their attention to the blazing of trees which marked the route and never rode close enough to make it obvious what tree I was looking at. They thought I was navigating by compass only and were impressed by my frequent halts to check bearings. I was far from confident that I could find Pedro's body again until I had a glimpse of ferns and knew that I was approaching the well glade.

My sharp turn to the left without any apparent reason made the Dominican suspicious.

"I should like your instructions for the return journey," he said.

"In case anything happened to me? Just go east!"

It was the edge on his voice which first made me realize that I held all the cards. I don't suggest that they were not brave men. They were. I should never have the courage to fight as an outlaw with a merciless army looking for me. But since they lived on their nerves uncertainty affected them.

When I picked up the natural avenue which led in the direction of Pedro's body I immediately turned away from it and rode through the trees along its line. From that angle it was impossible for them to notice that the avenue was there at all.

This was too daring. I went badly off course, and the avenue was irrecoverable. I was so bushed that I refused to trust the compass. Normally I ignored the slight deviation caused by my rifle and machete, since it was a constant, but I wondered if the weapons of my companions, riding as close to me as they were, could have thrown the reading out too far. So I dismounted, laid my machete on the ground and went off a few yards to take a bearing.

The Dominican picked my rifle out of Tesoro's saddle holster and said with pretended politeness that he would carry it for me. So I, equally politely, smashed our only compass against my right spur. That ensured that I should come out of the forest alive, whatever their reaction might be when faced with the remains of Pedro.

"From each according to his abilities; to each according to his needs," I said. "And I need my rifle."

The Colombian ordered his friend to give it back and reproached me for my lack of trust. I think he was sincere, but he had shown no sign of disapproval. A commander, I suppose, hesitates to overrule his security officer.

As the compass, before I destroyed it, had proved to me that I had managed to turn myself inside out, I rode on slowly until we crossed the avenue. It was then simple to pick up and follow my former route until I caught sight of the gleam of bone.

They examined the corpse like the experts they were. It fell in a heap away from the tree. The last insects left the joints.

"How do you know this is Pedro?" the Colombian asked.

[117]

"Because I recognize his revolver and belt. Because the skeleton has only been stripped bare very recently. Because no one else has entered the forest."

"The llaneros of Santa Eulalia?"

"They do not dare."

"Why not?"

I was not going to tell him about the pygmies, so I elaborated one or two of Joaquín's cautionary stories. Among his better duendes were ghost jaguars. Since their roar had been left behind in this world, all they could manage was to whistle and mew. Shortly afterwards we heard the piercing wail of an agouti. It was far away, possibly as far as the edge of the well glade, but the tenuous sound cut the haunted silence at a most convenient moment.

I was interested to see that the Dominican forgot he was a Marxist and involuntarily crossed himself. Likely enough poor Pedro, looking a traditional ghost in the half light, had carried him back to childhood fears of voodoo and zombies. Atheism is all right for the white-collared technicians of an urban society, but religion tends to reappear when threatened by ghost jaguars.

"Indians?" the Colombian asked.

"There are none."

The two wounds at the back of the skull puzzled them. They agreed that Pedro would instantly have crumpled up at the first shot, so why the second? If it was fired to finish him while he was on the ground, the shattering of the bone would be markedly greater around one hole than the other; if it was fired from the same distance as the first, Pedro must have turned his head while falling.

"Machine gun?" I suggested.

They thought that must be the answer, but who the hell could have automatic weapons except I or my unknown friends?

They still, I think, wanted to believe that I had killed Pedro; but nothing made sense. Instead of blaming it on the llaneros I had insisted that they were innocent. Besides, I had shown them the body when I could have denied any knowledge of Pedro's fate. And my firm belief that they had done the deed themselves must have appeared sincere.

"If you two didn't execute him," I said, "you had better consider some of your friends."

"Have any of them been seen here?"

"Never."

That started an argument between the pair. They agreed that the air attack on the herd was probably due to some big-mouthed partisan talking in the villages and a Government spy passing on the good news. As regards Pedro, they grew heated.

"Not even in Dominica would Pedro be considered worthy of death on no evidence!" the Colombian exclaimed.

The other retorted that in Dominica they were not

accustomed to have time for mercy. That was how I learned what his nationality was. But neither of them ever gave me their names or nicknames.

Whatever it was all about, I was at last in the clear. So I was prepared to lead them out. If it had seemed to me that Chucha and I were in any danger, I should not have hesitated to gain valuable time by losing them in the forest, even though it meant losing Estrellera and Pichón as well. They might or might not have found out which was east. Even if they did, the chances were that they would have borne away to the right and ridden in circles or perhaps — if they had the sense to give the horses their heads — arrived at the Guaviare and water.

In spite of having no compass I found the way back to the llano in three hours with hardly a check. It was, after all, my fourth journey. I discovered that I could now navigate by the contours and appearance of the roof above me as well as by trees which I recognized.

When we had crossed the creek I asked them if they were now satisfied and would leave me in peace to get on with agricultural development.

"We have no proof one way or the other," the Dominican answered.

I pointed out that I certainly was not a friend, but that he did have proof I was not an enemy.

"If I were a Government agent I could have got rid of you twice today," I said.

"Twice?"

"I was brought up never to point a gun at anyone — even when extracting it from a haystack."

The Columbian laughed and remarked that the only thing he was sure of was that in any circumstances I should do exactly what I pleased.

"Well, if you know that, we can understand each other," I said. "Sometime soon I shall be asked what happened to Pedro. Both the Intendencia and his wife have to know. I shall report precisely what happened, including your last two visits. The first visit is our own business, for you were my guests. I shall also say that I believe neither of you were responsible for Pedro's death."

The Dominican pointed out that Bogotá would know their identities from my description.

"They will know which two we are," the Colombian corrected him, "but not our identities — unless they have them on the file already."

They went straight off in the jeep in order to put as much distance as possible between themselves and Santa Eulalia before nightfall. The Dominican still distrusted me. If ever he comes here without his boss I should be wise to shoot him first and think afterwards. But I know I cannot do it.

Mario and Teresa hate the pair of them. They are instinctive individualists. If they could express their politics — which they can't because they haven't any — they would be anarchists. Chucha, however, is entirely reconciled to my two so-called friends, having listened to their conversation while I thought she was deaf and dumb with self-consciousness. She said they were good men who were persecuted. How could it be wrong to risk one's life in order that everyone should be equal?

I did not attempt to answer that. She might have understood if I had preached that the end did not always justify the means; but to explain why the end could never be reached at all was too difficult. Her simplicity is utterly different from that of Pedro and almost religious in its anxiety for the helpless. I wonder what would have happened if Karl Marx had founded his fantasies on primitive Christianity. Hippies in place of political economists?

This is all to the good because I can now allow her to think that my absences are due to close collaboration with these heavily armed saviors of mankind. I hope she never tells Valera so, or I shall be in trouble with the Government as well.

[*April 24, Sunday*]

Today I set out on Estrellera, taking my only other compass which is hardly more than a toy; but since I am not surveying, merely searching at random for signs of unknown pygmies, it is good enough.

When we reached the end of the long glade I hobbled the mare and turned her loose to graze while I scrambled up the low barrier cliff. From the top I could identify the sloping rock where I had laid out my presents, but it was far away and the green square of nylon was invisible.

Progress along the length of the ridge was out of the question. Thick scrub and badly eroded ground. Since nobody knew where I was or ever would, any accident such as a broken ankle could be deadly. So I remounted Estrellera and explored new ground, following the southern escarpment of the ridge.

There at last was game. I heard the distant rustling and clicking of a herd of peccary and caught a glimpse of a great anteater. Then, when I was searching on foot for a route to the ridge I put up a swamp deer and dropped it with a fluke of a snap shot right behind the shoulder.

This proved that there must be marsh or a small tributary of the Guaviare somewhere near and probably more breaks in the forest cover. A vegetarian tribe of dwarfs, living on roots and whatever fruit the monkeys dropped from the trees, always seemed to me most improbable. That hypothesis might now be rejected. If they existed, they were hunters. A game warden or zoologist could probably gain some clue to their movements from the presence or absence of the peccary, but I have no experience.

After lashing my deer on Estrellera, I found a ravine up which I could lead her as far as a patch of dappled sunlight. The going was easier than on the northern side, but I was floundering about for over an hour before I reached the flat rock. The nails and beads were undisturbed. The dried fish had gone, which was not surprising. Vulture or tayra or any of the forest rats could have taken it.

The silence on the top of the ridge still brooded, but I was not at all afraid as I had been on my first visit. Then the loneliness of the place possibly affected me. Now, the presence of abundant life in the forest below and the exhilaration of killing my deer stone dead without conscious sighting of the rifle gave a saner self-confidence. One must obviously be cautious among all these holes and boulders, especially when confined in a narrow cleft between rocks, but I have not seen or heard anything bigger than a beetle.

Home without incident. I must have traveled nearly thirty difficult miles. I asked Chucha if she minded being left alone all day. She looked blank. She had never conceived any other possibility. Men work and women stay at home. So they do, for that matter, in London. My question reveals a slight sense of personal guilt, as if I *ought* to remain with her when I have nothing to do instead of dashing out to play golf with dwarfs.

She is not idle. She helps Mario to carry water, and she is cleverer than he is at digging and closing little irrigation channels with the hoe. Her lime sapling, which she treats as her personal baby, is doing miraculously well. The fruit is to be for me. I should be worried if I really believed she was thinking that far ahead.

But she doesn't. The fruit is a child's dream gift, and has nothing to do with time.

Within the walls our personal food crops flourish, but all my experimental plots have had it. Grasses, wheats and leguminosae are dead except those which live under controlled conditions (see journal, p. 87 & notes). So my professional work is limited to an hour a day, and the only restriction on my explorations is that I refuse to be too tired at night. She is more desirable than ever as her confidence is freed and her youth dances. She will never be a sensualist. Too loving. Her sexual excitement, which becomes more frequent, shakes her but is quiet. A profound giving rather than a desperation.

Where the devil are the rains? With reasonable luck we should have had the first storms. My prospective little laborers can be of no immediate use now. But next year?

[*April 25, Monday*]

Today I took Chucha into the forest. I shall not take her there again until I clearly understand what danger, if any, it holds.

During last week I was not able to give enough time to her riding. If we ever had to get out of here in a hurry, it would be on Tesoro and Pichón with Estrellera for a packhorse. That would be a lot safer than a canoe out of Santa Eulalia. I don't know the shoals and rapids, nor how long it would take us to reach any sort of settlement.

She has a good seat and is getting on well. Pichón, like an old soldier, is inclined to take advantage of her gentleness. Today he nearly bucked her off just to see what would happen. What did happen was a beauty from me on his fat quarters. Chucha must learn to use the quirt herself when required.

After a few exercises we cantered straight across to the forest, entered through my first passage and then struck northwest. I had not intended to go so far from the grass, but a fearsome tangle of lianas forced us away into the big timber. As a result of her travels she was able to put a Spanish or Portuguese name to birds I did not know and to identify several small noises in the treetops. She also spotted rubber.

When we had ridden four or five miles through the darkness, the big timber opened out gradually into beautiful parkland without any definite wall of low, impenetrable growth. Here was a deep bay of the llano with what will be splendid grazing after the rains. Some small deer were over on the far side, extremely alert so that we only got a glimpse of them.

The going was safe, so I let her canter across the bay. She pulled up — or Pichón did — where the trees began to thicken again. I was tempted to show her what my intelligent Tesoro could do: gymkhana stuff which both he and I enjoy. Given his head he will go through

timber, zigzagging like a startled snipe, seldom needing
a touch and obeying it instantly. This time I was paid
out for exhibitionism. He shied so violently that I nearly
went over his withers.

What alarmed him was the carcass of a big bullock,
lying half in and half out of a clump of thorn. There at
last was certain evidence of jaguar. The neck was dislo-
cated, the ribs were broken and one hindquarter had
been completely torn off. The skin, where it was exposed to the sun, was dried and hard. Back and rump
showed the stripes of the claws where the jaguar
landed. The forepart of the beast was picked nearly
clean. Rats and a largish lizard — of some species
which I do not know — were worrying at the remaining
flesh under the safety of the thorns.

There was still a noticeable furrow in the grass along
which I assumed the jaguar had dragged the haunch. I
told Chucha to wait for me well out in the open and
followed up the trail with some vague hope of getting a
shot, though the jaguar must have finished his meal
days earlier and would now be far away looking for another.

What I actually reached was the scene of the crime,
showing that I do not yet know enough to be sure which
way an animal went, towards me or away from me. The
bullock had charged into the thickest stuff he could
find, going through it like a bulldozer in the hope of
scraping the jaguar off his back. Further on, a patch of
shrubby growth twenty yards across was beaten down

in evidence of the fight. The jaguar must have been very hungry to tackle the bullock at all, a much heavier and more powerful beast than the peccary and deer which were his usual prey. He had at last killed it, eaten what he wanted and then dragged the whole beast into the thorns.

I returned to the kill to see what more I could discover. Since he had not left the remains of the haunch at either spot, he must have taken it with him. It looked as if he had been disturbed while in the middle of breakfast.

Unless he had taken to the open llano, which was unlikely, there was only one way he could have gone: through a marked tunnel in the forest wall, which on that side of the bay was thick. I could not tell whether he made the tunnel or merely used it. It led me on hands and knees back into the forest. And there, not more than fifty yards from the outside world, were the haunch and the jaguar.

The accident which caused his death seemed obvious. He had jumped for a branch some twenty feet above his head, using the trunk of the tree to get there as the slashes made by his hind claws revealed. The branch had broken and was hanging down. It was an odd way for any cat to die; they do not misjudge the strength of branches, and even a heavy jaguar, powerful enough to drag a bullock, would surely only be winded by a fall onto softish ground. He might have intended to store the haunch in an upstairs larder, but its position some little distance away suggested that he had dropped it before he jumped.

Birds had torn open throat and belly, but had by no means finished their job of clearing up. Curiosity compelled me to brave the stench. When I examined the back to see if it had been broken by the fall I felt a sudden revulsion as if an agile centipede had threatened my hand. It was overwhelming surprise rather than nervousness. The jaguar's death was similar to Pedro's, though not an exact parallel. The beast had been shot from the flank, either on the ground or in the act of springing. The bullet had pierced the spine at the top vertebra rather than the base of the skull, and there were two neat wounds. This could be meaningless coincidence. I think it was. The projectile had probably been deflected by the skull and emerged nearly opposite to the wound of entry.

Two possibilities presented themselves: (1) that the pygmies had developed a far more efficient bow than other Indians — a weapon at least equivalent to the old English longbow and war arrow — or that they had a heavy spear and spear-thrower. Alternatively they netted their game or entangled the legs with bolas, then despatching even such dangerous enemies as the jaguar and Pedro with dagger blows at the base of the skull; (2) that somebody in fear of his life from Government or guerrillas was living in the forest and competing with the other carnivores for food. He was evidently a first-class shot and would not go hungry. He

[129]

may well have wanted a steak of that fresh-killed beef.

The latter hypothesis seems the more likely. Pedro mistook him for one of the llaneros, took a shot at him and was instantly killed in return. On the other hand Mario, Pedro and Joaquín have all talked of dancing dwarfs. If I reject this story entirely, I fall into the common scientific error of postulating a complicated cause when the available facts point to a more simple and elegant solution.

I went back for Tesoro and then joined Chucha on the llano. She had not been at all alarmed by the carcass of the bullock, which was as it should be. She was familiar enough with the remains of beasts stranded on the river sandbanks along with other flotsam. When I told her of the dead jaguar, she was eager to see it. There may have been a purely Indian touch of triumph over the dreaded enemy.

To avoid the labor of cutting a way for the horses we rode through the border of parkland on the south side of the bay and then made the circuit through the trees. When at last I found the animal, nose helping where eyes failed, I asked her if she thought it could have been killed by Indians — on the off chance that she might have heard how the river tribes tackled a jaguar. She did not know, but believed they would have cut out the claws for personal decoration. She made the intelligent suggestion that the holes might have been made by a vulture hammering with its beak to get at brains or marrow. Not a bad theory for the jaguar, but I won't have it for Pedro. His wounds were too neat.

She never questioned my explanation, backed up by the broken branch, that the jaguar had been killed by its fall. She took the episode as a mere casual curiosity. It looked as if I had cured her of any obsession with dwarfs and duendes.

On our way home I noticed that the merciless, lunar heat of yesterday and today had put end to the creek. It was a checkerboard of cracked, dried mud as hard as a brick pavement. Even the horses left no recognizable hoof-marks. I wish now that I had regularly ridden up and down the banks while there was still enough mud to show tracks. That would have been more sensible than searching the forest at random. Perhaps I have accepted too readily this won't-cross-water stuff. One is hypnotized by the desolation of the llano in the searing sunlight. Even at night I have seen no animal life but one agouti and one puma/dog.

Early tomorrow I shall ride to Santa Eulalia, leading Pichón, and see if I can persuade Joaquín to come out. He has not been here for weeks. There are untranslatable scufflings in the dust which may mean something to him.

[*April 26, Tuesday*]

A more or less successful day — though Joaquín is firmly set against any suggestion of small, bare feet and will not discuss the unmentionable. The trees are too near to talk indiscreetly about duendes, which do not, anyway, leave visible tracks.

Chucha was far from impressed by him. Joaquín is the last ragged remnant of the shamans of primitive food-gatherers, whereas she descends from the Children of the Sun. She does not herself express the difference like that, since in fact she knows far less than I do of her Peruvian ancestors. She merely says that Joaquín is a filthy old pig who is too fond of the demon rum. He is a pig, but a most interesting one. I suppose one must be secure upon the heights of civilization before one can start stirring up the bottom levels with profit and pleasure.

As soon as Joaquín arrived I had to feed and mildly intoxicate him. What he wanted was to eat food from cans, especially the more colorful and tasteless American emergency rations. With such luxuries about, it was no use to offer him a steak of swamp deer, lovingly tended by Teresa over a charcoal fire and brushed with chili sauce from an old tobacco tin. I was compelled to wait patiently until he had stuffed himself and slept, so we had no time to go far up or down the creek.

His examination was impressively professional. He translated the scuffles in the dust as rats and a capybara — which had been lying in the rushes for some time until it finally decided to get the hell out into the damper forest. I gathered that I was a disgrace for not shooting and eating it. I have never even seen it.

No deer. No peccary. Remains of a porcupine which had been turned over on its back by somebody's quick and daring paw and eaten out. Joaquín thought one of the smaller felines was probably responsible. He showed me a snake track which had ruffled the surface of the creek more plainly than feet, and told me how I could distinguish between the venomous snakes and the constrictors. The slow wriggles of the former made a wider path than the fast, hunting wriggles of the latter.

He also found the light imprint of a biggish clawed foot in what had been mud a few days before. Not puma, he said; it was an animal which chased its prey rather than stalked it, because it had five digits. It could be the track of the giant Brazilian otter, he thought, and the web might not show. I again talked around the question of dogs, not mentioning duendes but knowing that Joaquín would remember my inquisitiveness of two weeks earlier. He refused to be drawn, only saying sententiously that dogs could live tame or wild.

When we got back to the estancia he distinguished himself by asking if I would give him Chucha when I left. He reminded us that his wife was dead and proudly patted his pants, assuring us that he had an excellent erection as well as a house. He was prepared, he said (being now full of rum) to fertilize any of my laboratory plants which needed such intimate magic. Before Chucha's arrival I should probably have encouraged him to go ahead and measure results, if any. But simplicity in the male is not so attractive as in the female. I may be wrong in calling it simplicity. Joaquín's ritual mating with food plants is religious and therefore essentially complicated.

I had to get him away in good time. No estancia after dusk for Joaquín! He fell off twice on the way back, quickly remounting in case he should go to sleep where he was. Then I rode Pichón home through the early night, leading Estrellera. That's forty-eight miles in the day, and they are only healthily tired. Mario is at his old tricks again and insists that I must not travel after sunset. He gave me the impression that there was still some part of the Manuel Cisneros story which I have not heard.

[*April 27, Wednesday*]

A statement of intention to be compared with what actually happens — generally a source of amusement and disillusion!

It is obviously useless to spend a night in the pitch blackness of the forest, and explorations by day very possibly frighten away whatever I am trying to find. If I want to catch Homo Dawnayensis going about his business, I must watch the border of forest and llano at dusk or dawn when its abounding life is active.

My choice would be the bay of parkland where Chucha and I found the dead bullock, somewhere within sight of that tunnel. But it would mean starting improbably early without any good excuse. Nearer home, just inside my first cut passage, there is a half dead caju tree choked by lianas and easy to climb. From the top I shall have a fair view of the llano and of patches of the forest floor between the trunks. Meanwhile Estrellera can graze in peace. She has no nerves and will reach up and munch any tall tuft of grass instead of shying at the rattle of the seeds like Tesoro.

I wish it was not necessary to lie, but for the time being it is. I have announced that I shall be off in the dark tomorrow morning to catch a morning flight of geese far up the marshes. Mario considers the east side safe. Actually — if one wades — it is the only dangerous place for miles. Electric eel and sting ray must be in a filthy temper, assuming they have tempers, at the shrinking level of the water.

Walking to the caju tree is too slow, so I must take Estrellera though I would rather not. There's a risk of her fetching up in a cooking pot if hunting dwarfs exist. Alternatively, if they don't, my hypothetical outlaw has an excellent chance of riding off to Venezuela. A corollary to that. If he wants to escape, why doesn't he sneak over the wall and steal a horse? Or is he a tropical Herne the Hunter who enjoys living where he is? Nothing makes sense.

[*April 28, Thursday*]

What you think your eye is recording has more relation to your beliefs than to facts. I had in mind, when I
wrote that, the forest duendes compounded of one half
vegetable and one half fear. So I must be very careful. I
think that what I have seen is conclusive, but the light
was bad, the foliage thick, and my excitement was so
mixed with cowardliness that I could not separate
them. Probably psychic researchers feel the same, and
therefore cold, material evidence is harder to come by
than it need be.

I started at 3:30 A.M., taking the 16-bore, chiefly
because I had to be seen carrying it when I returned
to the estancia. It is also a fast and deadly weapon for
self-protection at close quarters when loaded with
No. 2 shot. I wanted No. 4 for geese, but could find
none in Bogotá. No. 2 turns out to be right for medium-
sized ground game.

A half moon was setting which made it unnecessary
to use a torch until I was beneath the caju tree. There
darkness was absolute, and I had to show light in order
to see exactly where I was and what was inhabiting the
tree. I disturbed three or four marmosets which cleared
off with faint squeaks of protest. The only other sound
was of Estrellera crunching dead stalks a safe hundred
yards away.

It was still dark when I settled myself in a triple fork
of the tree some thirty feet above ground. There was a

very light breeze blowing from the forest, so that nothing could scent me or see me. I would of course have
been heard — but that was as likely to attract as to re-
pel any creature which lived by hunting. The first
chorus of birds began. Before the howler monkeys
drowned out all other sounds I heard the very distant
call of a jaguar and again that full-volumed, tenor
whistle which had puzzled me the first day on the ridge.

Life was all in the treetops except for doves and
finches working along the edge of the llano. There was
no ground game about at all. This should be significant,
but I know too little of the reasons why sometimes there
should be plenty and sometimes none. From what I
have read of Africa, a lion's kill does not frighten the
herds into running far; on the other hand hunting by
man can clear the district. But I doubt if any parallel
can be drawn. There are no herds under and just outside the trees but peccary.

Behind me to the east the gray light was growing. I
could not help suffering from a compulsive instinct
that I had been seen and that eyes were looking at me. I
reminded myself that a dozen creatures were probably
looking down at me from the roof of the forest and
wondering whether the very large monkey was harm-
ful.

I did not feel affected by loneliness as I had on the
north side of the ridge, and I can rule that out as a
cause of possible hallucination. If there was loneliness
it was nearer to the anxiety neurosis of a man in a fair-

ground, unamused by the racket going on around him and resentful of a crowd safe and completely unconcerned with him. Eyes were certainly unsettled by the impact on ears, so that instead of quiet, thorough observation, I was continually glancing upwards, at the same time trying not to move my head.

To my left I could see a lot of the forest floor before the tree trunks closed the view. To my right front was a nightmare of lianas, which could have passed as an abstract painter's impression of dying forest. No one who did not know the reality would guess that the bare streaks radiating down from the top left-hand corner to fill the whole canvas were photographically exact. The lianas, black, gray and dark green against a background of grays and blacks, fell straight as storm rain, then curving away from the trees to their own roots. Seen from my height the pattern was as complicated as that of a vast rush basket.

Beyond and through this tangle I twice thought I saw movement. Distance could not be estimated, for thin ropes and thick ropes were so intermingled that perspective was unreliable. When I spotted the duende, it was not less than thirty yards away. I could not have seen it at all unless at the same time it had been trying to get a clearer view of me. I was reassured by our common motive of curiosity. It was really there.

It was not a monkey. It was dancing up and down to look at me from behind liana stems which approached the horizontal. No American monkey would have done that, but would have pulled itself up by arms or tail. It was not the butt of a rotten liana in an inexplicable state of instability, for it had a face. It was a dwarf all right, but unfortunately I could never see the face in profile which would have helped me to decide whether he was as human as myself or somewhat lower down the family tree.

His ears were not prominent. He seemed to have a small beard, but the light was so bad that I could not tell its color or the color of skin. Height was impossible to judge with any precision. Assuming he was standing on the ground and that the rest of him was proportionate to head and shoulders I reckon height as not less than forty two inches, not more than fifty. The eyes were indistinguishable but the straightforward stare seemed to make binocular vision quite certain. The jack-in-the-box jumps were rather like those of a stoat or weasel popping up to get a view over intervening undergrowth. If that is the dwarfs' technique of hunting, one might easily get the impression of a dance. I may have been looking at two of them. I think now that I was.

It was my usually quiet Estrellera who demoralized me. There was a hardly perceptible freshening of the dawn wind. At once she neighed in alarm and was off across the llano with the painful, clumsy rabbit hops of a hobbled horse. Up till then I had been fascinated and half skeptical — still ready to accept one of the startling freaks of radical leaves which account for most duendes — but now I remembered that I was a sitting target against the gray gold of dawn and that, as Estrellera's behavior proved the dwarfs to be real, the missile which stopped a jaguar could be real too. Leaving that out, one of the normal weapons of the forest Indian is a curare-tipped dart shot from a blowpipe. A deep scratch, and that — at any rate for birds and monkeys — is it.

However, I had undoubtedly been seen, so nothing would be lost if I could summon up enough guts to show myself openly and emphasize my peaceful intentions. In case they knew what a gun was, I laid it across two branches behind me and stood up with hands spread out and down, which I hoped was an interhuman gesture that they would understand. I then beckoned to him or them to approach. I also threw down my machete and made faces to indicate that it was a present.

Nothing happened. I was aware of the utter inadequacy of my attempts to communicate, yet I suppose the Conquerors when meeting potentially hostile Indians could do little better. I kept telling myself that if anyone got up from behind the lianas to shoot at me I should have time to swing round the trunk into cover. It then occurred to me that any hunter, having once attracted attention to the lianas, would make a circuit into the open woodland and shoot from behind a tree. I had no possible cover from that side; so I forced myself to wave a hand and smile a sickly smile like royalty from a glass coach, shinned down the tree into the bushes and got out fast by the cut passage.

Estrellera was still legging it across the llano, which gave me an excuse to run after her. When I caught her she was damp with sweat and needed a lot of gentling before I dared untie the hobbles. Why on earth should she have been so terrified? For her anything vaguely human is a possible friend carrying possible nourishment. I have known her to extend her lips towards a large tame monkey in the hope of getting half his sweet potato. It was the monkey which was alarmed by her greedy and affectionate approach.

Do the dwarfs anoint themselves with jaguar fat or glands? An ingenious theory which would account for her instinctive dash away from the edge of the cover. My own sense of smell — invaluable for detecting fine botanical distinctions — is exceptionally well trained, but the richness of the forest border at dawn drowns all individual scents. I think that I did pick up a faint, musky effluvium, though I cannot be quite sure.

I did not ride home immediately since Mario and Chucha would have noticed that I came from the forest, not from the east side of the marshes. So I walked Estrellera along the wall of trees — well out of range — with the red ball of the sun now hurling its first heat at us. When we were south of the estancia and out of sight I crossed the creek. It is possible that the dancers were moving on a parellel course. The monkeys were certainly hurling abuse at something below.

Teresa's scrawny and hideous hens had been doing their duty while I was away, so there was an excellent and very welcome breakfast. My violent prejudice against canned foods admits one exception. American bacon is superb. Chucha wanted to know why I had no geese and why I came from the south. That was easy. I told her that I had slipped the wrong cartridges into my pocket and found it out too late; so I had gone down the creek in the hope of putting up a capybara in the rushes.

I had to open up a couple of cartridges and show her the difference between No. 2 and No. 5. She was not suspicious. The little love is always eager to understand what I am doing and why I do it, and I am as eager to satisfy her curiosity. Chuchas taught to university standard might be a greater gift to the world than wheats which resisted our extremes of drought and tropical rain. But one dream is as fantastic as the other. I doubt if I shall live to see the day when there are sheets of water above the dams and mile after mile of crops and homesteads on the llanos. And I wonder if the hunting ape which is me would not then be home-sick for the remembered heat and emptiness.

It occurred to me while conducting on the breakfast table our elementary demonstration of the weight and diameter of lead shot that there was an explanation of Pedro's wounds which neither I nor the two guerrilleros had ever thought of. If the weapon which killed him was a shotgun fired at fairly close range there would be nothing out of the ordinary in two pellets striking him simultaneously and side by side while the rest of the pattern missed. The same goes for the jaguar; but one must assume much heavier ball than that of any normal cartridge. This theory suggests an old muzzle-loader — just the sort of thing which pygmies would be expected to have. But how do they trade for powder and ball when nobody has ever recorded their existence? It won't do.

In the cool of the evening, some four hours ago, I rode out to see what had happened to the machete. I did not think that the dwarfs would still be in the neighborhood but, if they were, I should have plenty of warning from Tesoro. I should not get him anywhere near the edge of the forest without a major conflict of wills.

He showed no more nervousness than usual at leaving the llano. Beneath the caju tree my machete lay where I had dropped it. I put it back in its sheath and then explored on foot, leading Tesoro. The rush basket of lianas seemed to be the apex of a very rough triangle, stretching away to the northwest. Chucha and I had ridden along the inner side of it.

I found and closely examined the spot where the pair of little people had been. I could clearly see the top of the caju and the fork in which I had been sitting, but anyone eighteen inches shorter could not and would have to jump up and down unless he climbed onto the prostrate lianas and exposed himself fully. Nothing was to be seen, no tracks, no trace of cutting, no small possession dropped. The tangle was so thick that only a bird or an arrow could have reached me in a straight line. To arrive at the caju tree the dwarfs would have had to make a circuit through clean, close timber. I suspect that they were doing so — with what intentions one cannot guess — when my nerve broke and I took quickly to sunrise and the open llano.

More precautions for my own safety as well as more tact will be needed. I must assume that the pygmies have for centuries observed white men on their horses and Indians in their canoes and that contact, when there was any, proved abrupt and bloody. Take, for example, the melancholy experience of gorillas in Central Africa ever since Du Chaillu shot the first of them little more than a hundred years ago. Their opinion must be that we are barbarous apes who pay no attention to the civilized gestures of a decent and respectable paterfamilias. Has anyone ever been killed by a gorilla? Certainly not, provided he obeyed gorilla convention and retired when requested to do so.

I should try to encourage Homo Dawnayensis to visit us and then open communications while remaining in the shelter of the walls. I wonder if prime, fat duck would not tempt him.

[*April 29, Friday*]

I took the beginning of the evening flight and got a fair bag in time to lay out the gifts before it was completely dark. I spread out half a dozen duck on our side

tion into the silence. Whether it was a mystic peace or an animal peace I do not know, and it is possible that they are the same. I will call it a peace of Eden from which we could advance to the still wider unity of llano, forest and our neighbor the Andromeda nebula, in that clear air shaped rather than misty to the naked eyes.

Our mating was inevitable without definite approach from either side, then still, intense, utterly motionless. Why is there no word in English but the wretched "orgasm" which smells about equally of the medical school and the brothel? I have never known that a physical sensation so pure and immeasurable could exist, as if the spirit were using the body for its own purpose rather than the normality which is the other way round. Our reason for being part of the night was all forgotten since we were the young night itself.

A fine pair of nature watchers Chucha and I would make! When we returned to our bench as silently as we had fallen from it, they were there for us, but at the very limit of vision. The black outline of the rubbish tip was broken. We both saw the two torsos — though with no more detail than logs of wood — jumping up and down with the curious movement which could be a hunting technique or a primitive form of the dance.

I did not dare use a torch for fear of frightening them away. When they vanished behind the mound and did not reappear, I was about to attempt speech. Chucha actually did so, in a few musical syllables which I could not understand. She told me afterwards that it was

[146]

Aymara and that she was appealing to them not to be afraid. They were more likely to recognize Spanish than Aymara, but the gentle voice made her meaning plain whatever she spoke.

The scent had its usual effect on the horses, and I dashed out to restore confidence. Pichón was the craziest, trying to break out of the corral, a rail of which he had already smashed. The other two hate and fear the smell of the forest people, but by now must be more accustomed to it. I partly calmed them and then looked over the wall to see if our visitors were near. They were not, but I again glimpsed an indefinable patch of night cantering away from the direction of the rubbish tip. Cantering best describes the motion. The back of the shadow, so far as it had any outline at all, seemed to be rising and falling more than that of a dog which stays fairly level. The felines come nearer to this flexible, concertina action and I should vote for puma rather than dog if I were not sure that this animal belongs to the pygmies.

[*May 1, Sunday*]

I have left Chucha to take her siesta alone. I wonder if she, too, feels that we have reached a summit of perfection which we shall never approach again. In God's name, why wouldn't she? But she would not leap to masculine immoderation as I do or ever admit, being a woman, that the future cannot equal the past.

[147]

That, however, is not the only reason why I have been sitting at the laboratory desk through the hours of heat. It is conducive to thought, and I must think urgently.

When the sun rose, Chucha and I went out to see what had happened to the peace offerings. The feathers of some of the birds were slightly disturbed, but that was all. Though birds are a major item in the diet of all forest peoples, there could be several explanations of why they did not take them. The wild fowl of the llano might be unfamiliar. Or they might consider them carion, possibly poisoned. How were they to know that the birds were fresh shot and a purposeful gift?

But that was not my problem. What has been occupying my thoughts is the dog/puma. It could have no objection whatever to fat duck killed that very evening. Yet the dog did nothing à la Sherlock Holmes. Like a trained spaniel? Nonsense! The solution in the end stuck out a mile. There never was any dog/puma at all. What I saw on both occasions was a "dwarf" running. He must be an anthropoid which goes on four legs when in a hurry, or else an animal which stands up on two when looking over obstacles.

Once that is accepted, everything falls into place. But I have decided to say nothing until I am quite clear in my own mind. Meanwhile this diary alone will be the inventory of conjectures and material evidence.

Now that the creek is completely dry our friends can

stroll over any night to inspect us and leave no tracks. If
only I had realized earlier that my dwarfs were nearer
duendes — though solid enough — and that even two
weeks ago there were muddy patches to reveal where
they were crossing, I could have settled all doubts. This
may be a nightmare, but I am going to assume that
when Chucha leaned out of the window after that first
dinner she was spotted and stalked, and that the scent
of the horses has attracted duendes on several occasions to a likely source of meat.

I deduce considerable speed and courage, for the jaguar did not stand, preferring to leave its kill and snarl
from the safety of a branch. It may have been momentarily winded when the branch broke or it may have
been hurt in the struggle with the bullock; but still it
was a full-grown jaguar and it was killed by a bite
through the spinal column.

It is now so obvious — and always should have been
— that the two holes at the base of Pedro's skull were
not made by any bullets but by two slender and powerful canine teeth.

[*May 2, Monday*]

Yesterday before sunset I ordered Mario to stable the
horses in the hall at night as he had done when Valera's
party were here. Chucha has already announced that
we saw small Indians. She is more excited than afraid.

From her point of view they are nervous, pitiable little creatures who screw up their courage to look at the estancia and then run. I have let it stand at that.

Mario asked no questions, merely saying that he had heard the horses plunging and heard me go out to them. I suppose he and Teresa checked doors and windows and pulled the common blanket over their heads. It is plain that I can never call on him for help if needed. He is right. A machete would be a useless weapon in the dark, even if one forced attack from the front by keeping one's back against a wall.

Having admitted that precautions should be taken for the safety of the horses, I could talk more frankly than when I pooh-poohed all his dwarfs and duendes. It was essential to find out whether he knew any solid facts at all.

"Have you ever lost so much as a hen?" I asked.

"No, Don Ojen."

"Then why do you shut yourself up at night?"

"Because the master told me always to do so."

"What did he know?"

"It was just that the llaneros would not go into the woods after the cattle."

"Did they ever see what was taking the cattle?"

"It is said that Don Manuel did."

Always this exasperating "it is said!" I asked him what the llaneros themselves thought. He replied that they would not talk about it after one of them had been lost, horse and all.

[150]

"That bit of paper of yours — when did Don Manuel give it to you?"

"Before he rode away for the last time."

"He had ridden often into the forest?"

"Just as you do."

"The llaneros had left already?"

"You know it is hard to say if a llanero has gone or has not gone. Some stayed on the east side of the marshes and rode in for their food and money so long as we had some to give them."

"So Don Manuel tried to kill the dwarfs?"

"He never said they were dwarfs."

"Then who did say it?"

"Perhaps those who saw them. Perhaps Joaquín."

"Was Don Manuel's body ever found?"

"Who would go and look for it?"

"Yet apart from the cattle and one llanero who may have ridden off to find himself a woman, the dwarfs have never done any harm to anyone."

"Who knows?"

"Then why did Don Manuel tell you to shut yourself up at night?" I asked, returning to the only solid ground.

"Well, look! I will tell you his words. He said to me: 'Mario, my valued gardener, take this paper which says that if I do not return you may stay here. And if you do not cross the creek and shut your door tight at night, you and Teresa and the boys will never have anything to fear.' "

[151]

"How much of this have you told to the señorita Chucha?"

"I? Nothing! A wise man does not mention such things. But she is often with Teresa, and how should I know what women speak of?"

That means, of course, that all along Chucha has known much more of the disappearance of Cisneros than I ever did. When she told me that with me she was afraid of nothing, she was already convinced that there was a nasty something to be afraid of. I wish I were not her god. What have I ever done except to show a lost child that her individuality is as precious to me as her body?

Cisneros. Yes. He had to protect his livelihood and get his llaneros back. I don't know if he too had anything particularly valued in the estancia itself. At any rate he was confident that stout doors and shuttered windows were enough.

Since the rains and a full, roaring creek cannot be much more than a week away, I should perhaps be content to leave the forest to itself and to accept that blank spot which haunted me for so long. But I am not content. Damn it, I am a scientist of a sort! It is my business to add to knowledge.

I rule out any form of anthropoid ape and any Lost World stuff. I do not yet rule out pygmies, remembering stories of Leopard Men. I think they went on all fours to kill. Even if I am wrong in that, there is no form of ritual killing which human beings haven't indulged in.

War, after all, is at bottom a ritual with ever more ob-
scene ways of giving death.

Nor do I entirely rule out a whole series of coinci-
dences: that Pedro was in fact executed by guerrilleros;
that the jaguar was killed by a combination of a fall
and a bullock horn which had nearly but not quite sev-
ered the spinal cord; that among the score of species of
monkeys there is one which will come down from the
trees and on to the llano at night. Time in this emptiness is still geological. No Colombian or Brazilian who
has traveled the forests would lay it down dogmatically
that the giant sloth no longer exists. And what about
the mastodon, thought to be extinct before man crossed
from Asia? Yet there is now some evidence that it was
in fact tamed and used by the Mayas.

So I shall go ahead with an open mind. At the moment research in tropical agriculture is about as useful
as it would be in the middle of the Sahara; amateur research in zoology might as well take its place. I am convinced that the ridge holds the key. It is far from a
unique formation, but reasonably rare. The cover and
shelter of those overgrown rocks with long glade below,
parkland to the north and more parkland lower down
the creek, all supporting game, make an excellent base
for a carnivore.

[*May 3, Tuesday*]

I had to take a horse — since my little world would have asked too many questions if I started out on foot — so I rode Pichón till I was near the edge of the forest and out of sight of the estancia. Then I hobbled him and left him well out on the llano where he would be safe till evening.

My original passage under the caju tree offered a much quicker route to the glades and the ridge than the blazed trail further south leading to Pedro's body. I forced a new way into the well glade without much difficulty and slashed down the ferns so that I should be able to recognize it on my return. Once I had passed from the well glade into the long glade I was much slower on foot than riding, but I lost less than half an hour in all and avoided the responsibility of looking after a horse as well as myself.

I made myself comfortable on top of the low cliff at the western end of the glade. Since I had learned that anything white catches the eye in the forest, I kept my face well under cover of leaves, picking off enough to give me a view of most of the glade on one side and the flat rock on the other. I did not expect to see a "dwarf." I might have to wait weeks for a clue to how and where they can be observed in daylight. But I did hope that the movements of game would give me a line, although I know far more about the trees themselves than what lives in or under them.

I had the Lee-Enfield with me — only as a precaution, for I did not want to shoot at all if it could be helped. Since range and accuracy were not of much value among trees, I loaded with a clip of dumdums. What I might need was stopping power at close quarters. The .303 bullet has little, unless perfectly placed. So I filed off the points of a whole clip, trusting that a dumdum would hit harder than a jaguar. I believe I must be right, but am still astonished at my train of thought.

The forest was very still: a few isolated bird calls, some small rustlings at the foot of my cliff, an old tree rumbling like a distant train as it crashed to the ground miles away. At twelve forty, when I had been in position a couple of hours, I heard the call which puzzled me the first time I was on the ridge, bearing south-southwest. It still sounded to me like sea gull or hawk, but of greater volume. It could be a jaguar cub's mew — I haven't the faintest notion what noise they make, if any — or just possibly a thin blast from a man-made instrument.

Half an hour later I had a fleeting glimpse of the black back of a tapir crossing the glade. Tapir do not move much during the day and hardly ever into sunlight, so it was a fair bet that he had been disturbed. But nothing followed him.

I gave up nature watching and came down from my perch. Then I worked round the end of the cliff and made my way along the northwest slope of the escarp-

ment on much the same line that I had taken with Tesoro. I admitted to myself that if I felt the same incipi-
ent panic as the first time on that desolate, ant-ridden,
overgrown tumble of rocks I was not going on.

In fact I felt nothing but growing curiosity. When I
was on the north side before, I was always looking
ahead of and around me. This time I had my eyes on
the ground and soon spotted that the ridge was not entirely lifeless. There were narrow, beaten strips which,
with a bit of imagination, one could call paths, but so
often they led to bare rock or lost themselves among
holes, pinnacles and thorny scrub that I was not dead
certain until I came across a dried dropping. It closely
resembled the puma/dog dropping on the llano. All I
could tell from it was that the animal was carnivorous
and that it ate little or no bone. It could be human.
Tracking was hopeless over leaves and rock. The sharp
slot of deer or peccary would have been distinguishable,
but not a spread foot or paw — at least not to me.
Joaquín, I am sure, could have told how his duendes
walked and on what.

I made a circuit in the general direction of the flat
rock, picking my way among the creeper-covered holes
and clefts where I ought to have put up or at least heard
some small creatures — armadillo, rabbit, lizards. But
there was no sign of life except the skeleton of some
kind of viper, of course picked clean by ants. Well
rooted in the silt at the end of a shallow ravine were a
few dwarf trees, among them a very fine flowering mi-

mosa. While I was working out a possible route to it I came upon the remains of another snake — this time a biggish boa about sixteen feet long. The back of the skull was pierced and partly crushed.

So that was the reason why there were no reptiles among rocks which ought to have been swarming with them. How difficult is it to kill a boa by clamping the jaws on the back of the neck and hanging on? I think any fast little carnivore could do it and that there is no need to postulate a heavy and powerful beast. This suggests that the killer could belong to the family of the Viverridae. Some of them do sit up on their haunches. But I don't see any sort of mongoose or civet cat tackling Pedro.

The rock was far away. I could make out my pitiable nylon still on top of it, plus a long, solid streak of bird dropping. One of the carrion hawks had probably come down in the hope of more dried fish and expressed his opinion when there wasn't any. Time was now running short and I had found out all I could; so I scrambled down to the forest, still seeing nothing but insect life. It is obvious that any creature unwise enough to live on the home ground of the duendes does not live very long.

I had left myself three hours to return to the llano before dusk, which was cutting it fine. Round the edge of the ridge and down the long glade was all plain sailing, but when I was under the big timber on my way to the well glade I walked fast and carelessly and bore a

little too far to the right. Finding that the borderline
vegetation did not appear where it should, I checked my
course by compass and discovered that I was heading
east all right, but that I had missed the well glade entirely. I should have been wiser to make a sharp turn to
the north and pick it up. That, however, would have
meant cutting still another way in — since I could not
expect to hit upon the fallen tree where both Pedro and
I had crossed from glade to forest — or making a difficult detour without any certainty that I would recover
my quick route to the llano. So I kept going.

I must have passed fairly close to Pedro's body. At
any rate I was somewhere to the south of the cathedral
aisle, for I was looking out for it and never saw it. I did
not for a moment feel lost, but unless I arrived at one of
the holes in the wall — a needle-in-the-haystack
chance — I could still be cutting my way out to the
llano long after dark. I had little fear for myself either
in the thick stuff or the open, and it is significant that at
this point I had complete confidence.

But to leave Pichón, hobbled and helpless, out on the
llano was asking for trouble — let alone little Chucha's
anxiety when I did not return before dusk — so I hurried on, bearing half left in the hope of catching sight
of one of my blazed trees or any other familiar landmark. All I recognized was the narrow path, a bit of
which I had crossed on the day I found Pedro. Then I
was not sure that it was a path. Now, after trying to
trace the same, vague beaten lines on the ridge, I had

no doubt. It seemed to choose a winding but purposeful route between the trunks. A compass bearing
showed that it was running more or less in the direction
of the estancia and that it could well lead to the liana
thicket. Once up against the impassable rush basket I
could easily follow the edge of it to the caju tree and so
out to catch Pichón.

I was soon sure what had made this faint ribbon of a
track. Twice I came on the familiar dropping among
the leaves. It then occurred to me very vividly that this
was the path which Pedro had crossed just before he
was killed. I must now try to analyze my odd and disgraceful behavior.

When I was up in the fork of the caju tree and found
myself under observation I was afraid of a missile —
more apprehensive, I think, of curare than of that improbably powerful arrow. It was a sane and logical caution exactly equivalent to that of some infantryman
who finds his cover not so good as he thought it was and
makes a dash for dead ground.

There was nothing logical, however, in my reaction
to the mewing call when I heard it not very far away —
possibly from near the edge of the well glade. It broke
my nerve and I started to run. I put it that way because
running was what the subconscious commanded. Physically, I did not do more than a jog trot. I told myself
that I must be getting along, that the sun would set in
half an hour. And I said out loud and firmly that the
call was a bird's.

[159]

The jog trot was quite enough to lose the faint path, which could only be followed by keeping the eyes steadily ahead and on the ground. If the forest had been completely open, I might be trotting still. As it was, I was halted by a dense stand of second growth and thorn. Covered with sweat, I took out the compass and had to put it on the ground because I could not hold it steady. I found to my horror that I had run in a half circle.

The shame of this — thank God for the higher centers! — pulled me together and I started off northeast: a course which had to bring me up against the rush basket, whether or not I ever recovered the game track. I hurried on, sometimes involuntarily running but always succeeding in checking and disciplining myself by a glance at the wretchedly wavering compass needle.

The only thing upon which I could congratulate myself was that I worked the bolt of the Lee-Enfield, ejected two rounds, examined them and reloaded. And I suspect that even that was not the cool precaution of a big-game hunter but merely another manifestation of panic. I had decided that the filing of the points might upset the spring and cause a jam. God only knows how it could!

There was no definite sign at all that I was being followed, beyond an imagined pattering over leaves which seemed to keep level with me far out to the left. So I started walking backwards until I perceived that it would not do me the hell of a lot of good. If I were going to be attacked from behind, my behind was wherever I chose to put it. Thereafter I made myself walk on normally, jumping round from time to time, until at last I came up against the wall of lianas.

I hit this at least a quarter of a mile further north than I should have done, but it was now easy to retrace my steps. My left flank was safe. Something might conceivably crawl under the rush basket, but nothing could charge or spring from it; so I had only a half circle to my right which had to be watched. I was still hearing soft paws, still pouring sweat, still stumbling about with the safety catch off and my left hand at the point of balance when the caju tree came into sight and I woke up from the nightmare. It was really like that. *Woke* is what I felt when I came out on to the blessed llano still lit, beyond the formidably long shadow of the forest, by the red light of sunset. Pichón was browsing peacefully on leaves not far away. He was listening with his great donkey ears, which meant little. His nose did not confirm my alarm. There was not even a ghost of a breeze to carry scent.

Now, what am I to make of this? If I were an Indian who had lost his head in this way, I should not only accept Joaquín's duendes but be certain I had seen them. Here in the green darkness, green whiskers. Among the myrtles of Greece, goat hooves and shaggy legs, Pan. Panic. Grendel in the Hall of the Sleepers. Which reminds me that I must double-check the hall of the horses.

As regards zoological research, am I now immunized against panic or am I unfit to be left alone in the forest without someone to hold my hand? Immunized, I believe. Let's not forget the snap shot which brought down that swamp deer. If I can keep my wits about me and have fifty feet of warning I am the quickest and surest giver of death in the forest. Singing in the dark? Well, my woodcraft may be lousy but I do know that my shooting is good.

Chucha has been communing with her sapling again. She notices everything. She might have seen Pichón out on the llano. It is also possible that her curiosity about No. 2 shot was not wholly disinterested.

She accepts, of course, that there must be mysteries. My past, my work, my relations with the outer world are beyond her sharing. But I think it likely that she knows from my eyes and expression when she has taken second place — momentarily — in my present life. Then, since she has nothing else but me, the sapling-teddy-bear has to be implored.

Never mind! Tomorrow I shall spend all day with my golden child. After that we'll see. I might ride into Santa Eulalia and buy a bullock.

[*May 5, Thursday*]

I spent a profitable day at Santa Eulalia — if it works
out. I found that the Government Canoe had come and
gone days before, and that there were letters for me
with the blacksmith. Pedro would have sent someone
out to warn me that the canoe was expected. Not that it
matters. I have no urgent wants.

The smith, Arnoldo — what names they have, going
right back to medieval Spain! — has taken Pedro's
place by tacit consent as head of the community. He is
slow and of dull intelligence. He cannot send out orders
by the canoe because he can't write, has never more
than a week's money and anyway is appalled by the
thought of shopkeeping. He has an immense store of
old and rusty iron, some of which may have been on the
spot since the first smith of the Conquerors crossed the
plains and could go no farther. So he can keep our
horses shod indefinitely. Saddlery and ropes, however,
will run short. Pedro kept a small stock, together with
bits, straps, buckles and silver decorations for the head-
stalls; and two or three of the llaneros who were clever
with their hands could make up whatever simple tack
was required — usually of rawhide, and often with
some individual touch of craftsmanship.

Tesoro's hind shoes had worn paper thin in the last
weeks of drought, so I left him with Arnoldo while I
read my letters. He is a very vain horse, always holding
up his head as if he carried a king, and Arnoldo tells

[163]

him that it is an honor to shoe him. So they get on well.

It is still difficult to adjust myself to the erratic mail. The Director was acknowledging and commenting on reports which I sent up to Bogotá with Valera over six weeks ago. Valera had, I gather, delivered my stuff in person and given a somewhat too romantic picture of my life as a llanero-agronomist. He had promised all the help that the army could give. That must have sounded as if the sky was going to be full of helicopters. What he meant — for his private amusement — was Chucha.

Another letter was only fifteen days old. The Director was anxious because nobody could communcate with Santa Eulalia. Remembering Pedro's unintelligible messages, he told me that if I merely transmitted the word AVION he would arrange for a plane to call and fly me up to Bogotá. Well, the canoe will have reported that Pedro's store has been burned down and that I, according to Santa Eulalia gossip, was in the best of health and very satisfied.

The Director also mentioned a mysterious and complimentary letter from headquarters of the National Liberation Army informing the Mission that I had nothing to fear and could continue my work in peace. Military Intelligence had confirmed that the letter was genuine and was furious at such impertinence. I was warned that the insurgents were killers first, foremost and all the time, and that I should trust them no more than mad dogs.

Bogotá! I am glad that I have no way of summoning that plane. I cannot leave Chucha here alone, and if I took her along what would she make of a Bogotá hotel? And what would friends and colleagues make of her? Not that I give a damn! Valera or some other dissolute scamp would undoubtedly advise me how to handle a situation which cannot be unfamiliar. But, whatever I did, the coarse and the comic or the degradingly secret would be emphasized at the cost of all our delicious simplicity. The only pretense which could come close to our real relationship would be to pass her off as an adopted daughter. But that would mean laying off the child — which I can't.

No, I shall not go up to Bogotá till I have to. It occurs to me that I am very happy. Is the secret of happiness a mixture of passionate fornication and somewhat chancy hunting? If so, we human beings have been continually frustrated by urban life ever since we were fools enough to invent it. It's little wonder that some of us rush off to war with a sense of relief.

I slipped all this unimportant bumf in my pocket and strolled down to the river to see Joaquín. A medical consultation. Going through the fern and tall grasses into the forest and in and out of the glades I am showered with ticks and have to get them off when I arrive home with cigarette end or tobacco juice. Chucha's attentions to my back are charming and efficient, but waste a lot of time which could be better spent. Insect repellent is useless.

Joaquín greeted me with his usual impassivity and said that it gave him great pleasure to see me. This was exceptionally polite; indeed his tone was not conventional at all. So I asked him how I could be at his service.

"If you had been here, you would have bought me rum from the canoe," he replied. "But I speak of the day before yesterday when you were so afraid."

I asked him how he knew I was, and he answered that he had felt my fear.

"As for Pedro?"

These shots in the dark were so often effective.

"No, not as for Pedro. For Pedro it came quickly."

"Could you know whether I had died or not?"

"Not yet."

I think he meant that only when my spirit had recovered from the shock and was wandering about looking for something recognizable would it be prepared to enter his revolting haze of ritual smokes and incantations. But I respectfully record the shaman without trying to explain him. I doubt if the Archbishop of Canterbury's comments on a Mass for the Dead would be any more helpful.

I told him that I had seen his duendes and that they were solid as ourselves, though I could not yet put a name to them.

"How do we know what we are, we men? So how can we tell if duendes are the same?"

[166]

He kicked a log, exactly like Doctor Johnson refuting Berkeley, but drawing a different conclusion.

"Is my foot? Is the log? I only know what my toe feels. When we are afraid, that is the duende. That is what a duende is."

His Spanish is even worse and less intelligible than my translation makes it sound. Understanding of him is due to our deep curiosity about each other rather than to his actual words. But I think I am safe in putting his meaning this way. Panic always has a cause. Whether the cause has green teeth and whiskers or goes on four feet is irrelevant. The only reality is the fear.

Even now I have not got it right. I have made him too skeptical. He believes profoundly in an immaterial duende which lives on fear as we live on meat. Fear gives it an existence and a shape which is material enough to kill.

I did manage to mention the ticks. He gave me a dried gourd with some whitish goo in it which, he assured me, would make any tick let go and wither. He said it was also good for wasp stings and would restore virility in the aged if taken internally. He proposed to manufacture a new batch when I was ready to hand over Chucha.

When I went back to recover Tesoro I shared Arnoldo's dish of beans — having forgotten that one can no longer buy food in Santa Eulalia — and waited in the smithy on the off chance that one of the llaneros

[167]

might ride in. And what a good and ancient scent it was under the thatch — the charcoal, the sweat of men and horses, the sizzling of a generation of patient hooves! This is rich country for the nose: llano after rain, forest at dawn, sweet cattle, breath of Tesoro when we blow at each other muzzle to muzzle. And that is to say nothing of the musk of Chucha's damp body. It is a melancholy thought that the more successful I am, the more I help to drown the lot with the petrol and hot oil of the machine age.

I was still reluctant to say all I knew of Pedro. I shall report his death to the first official who comes along and I hope tomorrow or the day after to know the cause of it. So I switched conversation to Pichón and said what good care he took of my girl. Arnoldo told me he was nearly twenty — I had thought about fourteen — and sound as a bell. He had been left to Pedro by a llanero who owed the store money and was dying before he could repay it. They are either bandits or punctiliously honest. There seems to be nothing in between.

Alvar, one of the gentlemen who had chased Pedro to his doom, rode in when the heat of the day was fading. He had lost the silver rowel of a spur and wanted a new one. Arnoldo could only offer to file it from mild steel and said it would look like silver if regularly oiled. That didn't suit Alvar at all. Fortunately I was able to produce a silver dollar which Arnoldo could bore and file to shape. He was even going to line the hole with a bush to prevent wear.

Alvar insisted on paying me. Both of us knew that he had nothing looking remotely like money, but neither would ever have mentioned it. However, here was the chance I had been waiting for. I told him that a silver dollar was a trifle among gentlemen such as ourselves and that I had far more important business. Would he sell me a steer and deliver it north of the marshes?

He was suspicious, not knowing whose side I was on and afraid of getting a plane and machine gun all to himself. I swore that I was not reselling to anybody, and explained that I wanted to follow the steer about, see what it ate and find out if there was anything wrong with the grasses of the unused grazing between the marshes and the forest. He looked at me oddly, but evidently decided that it was not his business to mention dwarfs.

Tomorrow, two hours before sunset, the beast is to be delivered at a tall, solitary palm with an aloe growing alongside it, known to everyone as the Mother and Child.

On my return to the estancia I told Chucha and Mario that the canoe was expected daily in Santa Eulalia and that I should spend a night or two there so as not to miss it. Tomorrow morning I shall pack up rations for myself and Tesoro, though I hope I can persuade Alvar to lead him away before dark and bring him back when the sun is up. I don't expect any trouble and I am determined to take no risks, but I have left a note in my official journal that everything I possess on this side of the Atlantic — there isn't much but books on the other — belongs to Chucha.

[*May 7, Saturday*]

At four o'clock yesterday I found Alvar already waiting with a bullock in the shade of the palm. Though its horns were short for our local breed of cattle, white blotches on the flanks showed a not too distant Hereford ancestry. It would be easy, I thought, to see the beast at night.

The Mother and Child were all of five miles from the bay of parkland, about as near to the forest as the llaneros will ever graze their cattle. The horizon was a vast, unbroken circle, looking emptier than I had ever seen it. There was no haze over the marshes which were hidden by the slight folding of the ground. The line of the forest under the low sun could have been a streak of cloud.

I paid Alvar a small sum for the ownerless beast and he asked me, with much circumlocution, what I intended to do with it.

"We think you know already what is wrong with the grazing," he said, "since you have passed so many moments with Joaquín."

I told him frankly that I did know and that I intended to present the bullock to the dwarfs.

"They have had enough already," he answered sullenly.

"Perhaps this time they will have a surprise."

"You are as mad as Cisneros!"

"Did he go in with a bullock?"

"No, man! He was alone, they say. I tell you that neither you nor your beast will be alive by morning."

"If we are, you will also find a dead dwarf alongside us."

He was not impressed by this Castilian magnificence.

"I shall not go and see. Nor any of us," he said and turned his horse.

I started to drive my beast westwards. It preferred to go home to its herd. When I headed it off, it charged Tesoro who swung his hindquarters professionally — though he knew no more about the business than I did — and then put out for Santa Eulalia himself. While we settled our differences the bullock pretended to be grazing, and I had a chance to catch its fat rump a heavy cut with the quirt which shot it off towards the forest. It then trotted around, not knowing what to make of us, while I tried to get a rope around its horns. I couldn't handle the fellow at all. I remembered too late that the animals which they tie out in Africa and India are tame village goats and buffaloes, not an unmanageable Colombian steer.

Meanwhile Alvar was lying on his horse's neck, insane with nervous laughter. It had never occurred to him that a good horsemen, as he knew me to be, could not drive cattle. He took pity on me, and we set off for the bay of parkland at such a pace that I thought the bullock would die of heart failure before it got there.

It was now nearly dusk. He was far from laughter while he helped to tether my present for the dwarfs to the bole of a thorn. He took Tesoro and said that he would wait for me all the morning at the Mother and Child, refusing to come nearer. He did not even wish me luck. I was finished for him. The nearest I got to a good-bye was a whinny from Tesoro.

Since not a one of the present llaneros of Santa Eulalia has, so far as I know, ever seen dwarf or duende, the power of superstition is extraordinary. Long before Cisneros made his rash purchase of the estancia rumors or reports must have been lurking in the grassland like ticks, fastening on to the men as soon as they began to lose beasts between the forest and the water.

Alvar was in such a hurry to be off that I could spend no time searching for a better place to tether the bullock. The tunnel which I particularly wanted to watch was further on at the bottom of the bay. Since all the trees which overlooked the bait had smooth, unclimbable trunks, I had to be content with a conical termite hill, seven feet high and hard as concrete. I reckoned that if I sat still I could pass as an extra story on top. My back felt naked, but was partly sheltered by thorn and cactus. The breeze was uncertain but seemed to be settling to its usual pattern of forest to llano.

When darkness fell I soon grew impatient, and began to realize how hopelessly inexperienced I was. Starshine among trees was not sufficient to see more than a flicker of white — and that only by straining the eyes — where the bait was quietly chewing the cud. I had tied a pencil torch beneath the barrel of the rifle, but it was not much use. My left hand either had to move to switch on, probably losing the vital half second of opportunity, or it got in the way of the beam. As for sitting still on my termite heap, I could not do it. I envied the hunters of more imperial forests who could summon up natives to build a machan.

The local herd of peccary came out to feed on the edge of the forest, some of them passing close to my spire, which proved that my scent was not disturbing them. I could only just see them and they certainly could not see me. They must have heard me, for my thigh went to sleep and I had to change position. It may be that they put me down as a monkey or that they had never been hunted by man. I think the latter likely. I am on virgin soil, and the game is as ignorantly trustful as I am.

A half moon came up about two and enabled me at last to see the bullock. He had eaten the dry grass stalks in a beaten circle around his thornbush and was now lying down. I could have shot him neatly behind the ear. There was no need to use the clumsy torch.

The peccary moved off towards the middle of the bay, the nearest of them still in sight. A pair of owls flitted to and fro, passing low over me and the bait until they decided we were too large to be of interest. After half an hour the bullock got to his feet and started paw-ing the ground, with his head pointing across the bay.

What I now saw or half saw was out of pattern, for peccary are among the bravest and most formidable of any herbivorous animals. When in danger the whole herd will attack, and lord help the dog which cannot run faster or the man on foot who finds no handy tree! A shot in the air will usually turn aggressive cattle, but will not, I am told, turn a herd of peccary. If the intruder does not get off the premises, he will be under those razor-sharp little hooves.

A single peccary on the outskirts of the herd broke away and took off for the llano squealing as if the devil was after it. The herd neither attacked in its defense nor crossed its line. Indeed I had an impression — in which I put no faith although I could make out their backs in the long grass — that they actually moved off the line, leaving a space for the pursuer. It was behavior clean against the norm.

The following shadow appeared for a fleeting second as two loops. By the time I had decided that there could not possibly be a boa constrictor of that size and that no snake heaved middle sections of its body off the ground, the bullock had torn the inadequate thornbush out by the roots and was off to the llano as well.

I swung round to cover it and never had a second glimpse of the loops. I was pretty sure that what I had seen were the backs of two duendes in line chasing the peccary with their curious loping gait — in fact the sea serpent effect of two porpoises, one behind another, leaping simultaneously.

There was not another movement till birds and monkeys began their racket at dawn. I got down from my perch, stiff, bored, cold, hungry and not much wiser. Still, the duendes had only won the first round on points. The peccary gave away some of their habits. Its carcass was four hundred yards out on the llano with the vultures just settling on it. I drove them off before they could tear away the evidence.

The peccary had been killed by the usual bite. Two canines had met just below the skull. The other two had passed under the spine. That explained why both I and the guerrilleros, seeing only clean perforations in bone, had jumped at bullet wounds. There was not enough soft tissue left on either Pedro or the jaguar to show the damage done by the canines on the other side of the jaw.

The belly had been clawed open and the soft parts eaten. Teeth had torn open the jugular vein, yet there was no crusted pool of blood. I have a strong feeling that duendes not only draw their life from panic, as Joaquín suggested, but from the blood of the kill, sucked or lapped.

The bullock was a mile further on, still attached to its bush. It appeared to welcome my arrival, though not to the extent of standing to be patted. I left it to look after itself and walked on wearily over the llano to the Mother and Child.

[175]

Alvar turned up at ten with Tesoro and was surprised to see me. I wouldn't say he was pleased. Men are not when beliefs as well as caution are shown up to be exaggerated. No doubt he also expected to be able to keep Tesoro, who would never be much use as a cow pony but at least would win him some silver in bets if he cared to ride as far as Venezuela.

I said that the dwarfs had so frightened the bullock that he had torn out his bush and was now ranging the llano. Alvar asked if I had seen them, to which I replied that I had even seen them dancing and that I hoped to persuade them to work on my irrigation channels. I shall not give it out that they are animals until I am dead certain what they are. Meanwhile let it be dwarfs with whom the learned doctor is nearly on speaking terms! That cuts them down to size and might enable me to get some active help if I need it.

I told him to take the bullock back to the herd and keep it for me. I do not think I shall want it again. This sitting up over a beast is a romantic idea borrowed from books. To be successful one would have to know far more about the habits of the creature one is observing. I had amazing luck in making contact at all, due to my hunch that the bay was regularly hunted and that the tunnel was their way in and out of the forest wall.

The next move must be to try to get a sight of this pair on their home ground in daylight, and I must not play their game when I "feel" their presence. I believe that Joaquín is on to an actual fact related to their method of hunting and general ecology. They produce what one might call a Declaration of Intent which is detectable by horse, man and even jaguar, to say nothing of peccary. So does man himself. His murderous presence signals a warning to all his four-footed cousins, and nothing but a tired, old man-eater will call his bluff. So I hope I can safely assume some timidity in the duendes, or at least the normal strong objection to starting trouble. Pedro's death does not prove that he was deliberately chased and killed. More probably he took them by surprise on a track which they considered their own territory and did not retreat when told unmistakably to do so.

[*May 8, Sunday*]

When I rode in yesterday afternoon, supposedly coming from Santa Eulalia, I had no need to invent a story and truthfully said that the Canoe had called. I could not pretend it had not, thus leaving myself free to be absent from the estancia for more nights, since Chucha saw all the new letters I was carrying. I keep her out of nowhere and out of nothing she can understand. Love and youth are privileged.

I noticed a flicker of disquiet at the arrival of so much evidence that I had another, more permanent life. She can only guess at it, but of course she fears it. Sometime I have to go, and to what does she return then? I presume she thinks it inconceivable that I would hand her over to Joaquín, for that is a standing joke between us. But she must anticipate an end not far off Valera's solution: that she will be passed with a kiss and a dowry to some fellow like Alvar. I cannot bring myself to tell her that we shall never be separated. I wish I could.

There is no limit to the oddities of the sort of human thinking which isn't thinking. Mario, Chucha and Teresa now take the dwarfs as fact. Mario begs me to be very careful and gives me tips on how to approach un-tamed Indians. I am never, never to surprise them, he says. That goes for more than dwarfs.

He has been digesting the question I asked him: whether in fact the dwarfs had ever killed so much as a hen in or around the estancia. The answer is no. He even points out to me that all we know of Cisneros is that he was ruined and rode away. He may not have been killed by the dwarfs. He and his horse may be any-where in the Americas. Everything is turned a little too much upside down. It is now I who have to impress it on Mario that at night all doors and windows have to be kept shut and that the horses must never be left in the corral.

I have been right round the perimeter with him and insisted that adobe rubble on the outside must be dug away and piled on top of the wall. To avoid alarm I play up the new legend of the pitiable pygmy. Suppose the poor little sods, I suggested, came in to steal or kill horses and were surprised at the job. Then we might not be able to avoid mutual bloodshed and enmity. So keep them out till they know us better! He never asked why, if they are men, they cannot climb a half-ruined wall like ours. All the traditions of the duende remain in force, though the duende itself is exploded.

The mystery has grown up because — at any rate in the open — the duende is nocturnal, and the secret presence of a nocturnal animal can only be detected by its kill. The llaneros, since they stayed clear of the forest edge, very seldom saw a kill. When they did, it was unfamiliar and inexplicable, probably the work of man. Combine this with the rare glimpse of an upright figure in deep dusk and the terror of horses communicated to their riders, and there you have the origin of the dancing dwarfs.

My next problem is to find out where they drink. When the creek had water in it, they did occasionally come as far: the horses knew it if the wind was the right way. But they do not hunt on the open llano. That is certain. I think that they move out from the ridge in the late afternoon when I was stalked — or merely investigated — and that they watch the forest border when the game moves out to graze on what is left of the grass or to browse on leaves which the sun has packed with nourishment. Whether they kill within the gloom of the forest during the day I do not yet know. It looks as if they do, when tempted or disturbed.

But they must have water on their home ground. Blood alone is, I imagine, too salty to quench thirst. The big felines lap it as it flows, but appear to need water in large quantities. Obviously I have not been far enough into the forest. Somewhere below the southwest slope of the ridge must be pool or spring. The presence of that swamp deer proved it. And the tapir which I saw crossing the long glade must have cool forest water in which to drink and wallow.

Chucha and Pichón are now so sure of each other that she can ride with me to the new southern passage tomorrow and lead Estrellera home while I explore the swamp deer country on foot. She does not object so much as I expected to my wandering in the forest without a horse. She is conditioned by her whole life not to interfere with men's business. And Samuel of course always walked.

[*May 9, Monday*]

That has settled classification, though not much more. Without a doubt they belong to the family of the Mustelidae, not the Viverridae.

Through the leaves I watched Chucha ride away. She showed some signs of agitation — which she never does when I am with her — and took it out on Estrellera when the mare tried to get her head down to eat. There was no further question who was boss.

Starting from this now familiar entry into the forest, navigation was easy. The blazed trees led me straight to Pedro's body. I was very reluctant to look at it again, but forced myself to do so. The forest was beginning to clean up in its own way. The bones were already greenish in color. A Desmoncus liana growing in the well-fertilized soil had actually disarticulated and picked up the pelvis on its hooked spines, lifting it a foot clear of the ground. If the growth had been through the eye sockets of the skull, the macabre effect would have terrified anyone, Indian or not. I wonder if many of the duende stories may not be due to the fact that there are no wild dogs or hyenas in this country to destroy what the birds cannot crack or carry.

Since I knew that by walking due west I must somewhere pick up the escarpment of the ridge, I did not bother to take the long glade. The timber was big and well-spaced and the going easy, though melancholy, monotonous and oppressively silent. It was hard to believe — it always is — that a hundred and fifty feet above my head was sunshine so merciless that the domes of leaf and blossom were wilting and the tree dwellers asleep in the perfumed shade.

When I met rising ground I followed the contours, leaving on my right the ridge itself and the many ravines up one of which I had climbed with Estrellera. Eventually I was stopped by thickening ground vegetation, a sure sign that somewhere ahead the sun penetrated the canopy. I began to climb directly upwards in the hope that I should be able to see into the clearing from the top of the ridge and find an easier route to it.

The tangle of ground creepers and stone was the worst I had hit yet, especially difficult because I thought it wise to take the rifle off my back and carry it. I was moving across the herringbone of erosion, climbing down and out of one cleft after another. After three hundred yards of this — which took me nearly an hour — I saw a gleam of water below me between the leaves. Cutting a way to it over the flat was going to be quicker than scrambling across rock to the head of the pool or stream, so I took the first practicable ravine down to the forest and then continued westwards.

The ground became spongy and the vegetation mostly soft. One satisfying swipe with the machete was enough to bring down stems as thick as one's calf. I came out at last into the no-man's-land of swampy forest, where what you tread on may be a root, may be floating or may be mud.

I have never seen such a concentration of brightly colored life, animal and vegetable. The branches which hung out over the still water were loaded with epiphytes. There were yellow-flowering cassia, orange bignonia, several species of short-stemmed nymphaeaceae and a very fine purple ranuncula which may be unknown. Hummingbirds and green-and-blue tree creepers were everywhere, and there were enough butterflies to keep old Samuel busy for a month. Nature's passionate exhibitionism, always repressed under the trees, had been hurled on stage by the sun.

It was impossible to follow the shore of the swamp or to make out its general shape. However, a fallen tree offered a sort of pier running out a hundred feet into clear water. I tested it cautiously and found that it was not yet rotten enough to let me through or to be frequented by the varied and sometimes unpleasant creatures which make their homes in hollow trees. There was only a nest of hornets towards the top of a branch, which I was careful not to disturb.

From the end of the tree I had a view up and down the pool. I could see the stream which fed it and hear a fall tumbling down the lower slope of the ridge. In the rainy season the stream evidently burst out with sufficient force to clear all soil from a shallow rock basin just above the point where it entered the swamp. On one side was a beach of sand or mud which I intended to examine for tracks, but for the moment I was very content to sit at the end of my pier and watch, reckoning that if I kept still I could pass as a thick dead branch. The only animal life in sight — beyond insects — was a small and enterprising alligator. After all the noise I had made in cutting my way to the bank it was unlikely that I should see anything else for hours.

There was a very slight current, showing that the swamp drained into the Guaviare or a tributary. In the rainy season the width of the lower stream must be enough to stop the duendes crossing. That they do not in fact cross water has been pretty well proved by the creek. It follows that their permanent habitat ought to be on a watershed from which they can move in any direction.

The ridge meets their requirements. The faint runways bear this out; so do all those clefts and holes without even a guinea pig or reptile — snapped up for a snack in passing, with enough fragments left to encourage the ants. Additional evidence, for what it is worth, is my instinctive aversion to the ridge when I first visited the north side.

I had started from the estancia at dawn. It was now eleven. Since there was little cutting and no climbing to be done, I counted on getting back to the llano in three hours' hard marching. So I had four hours to play with. I ate my sandwiches and afterwards kept as motionless as I could in spite of the sharp plague of insects.

The afternoon wore on and the place returned to normal. A small brocket deer flashed in and out of sight as it jumped the stream at the head of the swamp without stopping to drink. A green tree snake moved cleverly from branch to branch looking for birds and small monkeys. When my ears had become accustomed to the background of buzzing and humming, the place seemed as silent as the forest. The steaming, lovely pool, under a blazing sun reflected back again from peacock-turquoise water, gave me a quite reasonable daydream that I was drowsily living in the Carboniferous and should be laid down among the leaves in a coal measure.

The duende called clearly from the ridge. It was close, not more than a hundred yards away, and did not sound in the least like a sea gull or any man-made pipe. It resembled the full-throated mew of an otter, though higher in pitch. I remembered Joaquín's doubtful identification of the faint print in the dried mud of the creek. He said it could be that of the giant otter, Pteronura Brasiliensis.

I watched the ragged skyline of the ridge wherever I could see it, but there was no movement. When my eyes at last returned to the swamp and its banks, the dance was in full progress, this time with only one dancer. It must have hunted my line through the bamboos.

It was inspecting me from behind the upturned roots of the tree, bobbing up and down. I saw how I could have mistaken the head for human, though it now seemed incredible. The eyes were round and set well forward, the ears hardly perceptible, the head held well up so that in bad light one could create for oneself the illusion of a man's neck. The muzzle was as pointed as that of a feline, but no more so. When seen full face, as a vague outline without any scale of reference, it had been easy to imagine something like a human nose and mouth and to mistake the slope of thickish fur on the broad, heavy skull for a forehead.

Dancing behind the root it made as easy a target as the head and shoulders which bob up and down on a rifle range. Naturally I never dreamed of firing on so handsome and presumably rare a creature. The round eyes also gave a disarming impression of innocent curiosity, as much as to say: what the devil are you?

This curiosity was not, I think, purely anthropomorphic interpretation. Since all their usual prey is four-legged, they could well be puzzled by a tall, slender upright animal with an outline closely resembling their own — making a false identification exactly like the Indians or llaneros who first saw them in dusk or darkness. This could account for the fact that I was undoubtedly hunted on May 3, but not attacked.

I saw a slight waving of the tops of the bamboos which indicated that it had moved out of the cover of the tree root and a little downstream. It then launched itself from what must have been a crouching position clear onto the fallen trunk with the peculiar loping leap which I had seen at night. It was a magnificent creature, pale fawn with a paler belly, standing about twenty inches at the shoulder. Length from head to root of tail approximately four and a half feet. Tail apparently short, but I never got a leisurely side view. Weight very difficult to judge because of the markedly lithe and slender build. For a loose comparison I should say it was longer than a jaguar (not counting the tail of either) but stood lower and was much lighter. It did not appear at all out of proportion or dachshund-like. It was as dangerously graceful as leopard or jaguar when they move with body close to the ground, but had shorter legs without the muscular striking power of the felines.

I record all this while the picture is still vivid in my

mind, but at the moment my observations were more of
character than measurements and were urgent. Another long bound took it out along the tree. When we
faced each other with a mere forty feet between us, its
curiosity did not seem all that innocent. It plainly had
no idea of what a firearm was and no fear of man. That
cut both ways. I had no way of quickly distinguishing
whether it was a beast which could easily be tamed and
domesticated (like the ferret) or whether it saw me as
helpless meat.

I myself was tense but not afraid. Its Declaration of
Intent had no chance to work when I had only to press
the trigger and rake it from stem to stern. It did occur
to me, however, that the head shot, which was the best
that offered, might not be effective. The tremendous
jaw muscles, which could drive the canines through the
base of a skull, were attached to a formidable ridge of
bone.

It had the extraordinary impertinence to pop up for a
better look. I could now see at close quarters how the
dwarf effect was produced. It sat upright, hind paws
and base of tail giving support at three points, fore paws
held close to the body and dangling. That made quite a
considerable pygmy. I had already formed the opinion
that it was one of the Mustelidae, and this trick confirmed the classification. Otter, stoat, badger, tayra —
they all do it.

Now undoubtedly gathering itself for the spring, it
crouched again. I was aiming straight between the eyes

[187]

when the hornets took a hand. The mustelid had put some weight on their private dead branch, which I had been most careful not to do. The swarm could make no impression on the fur but went for the nose and the belly, which suggested that this was the female of the pair with vulnerable teats, possibly nursing cubs. At any rate he or she was off to the bamboos again in two curving leaps with a cloud of hornets following.

It left behind a strong, not unpleasant whiff of musk: another proof that it was a mustelid. All of them, so far as I know, emit scent when at play or when alarmed, varying in power from the appalling stench of the skunk to the woodland smell of badger. It was evident that the hornets caused more alarm than I did. If jaguars will not tackle this fellow, the only other possible enemies are wasps, hornets and Eciton ants.

My guess — worthless until proved or disproved by anatomy — is that the duende and the giant otter had, a few million years ago, a common ancestor. One genus developed on the great rivers very successfully; the other not so successfully on land — perhaps because it grew too heavy to catch easy prey in the trees and so developed speed and killing power as a rare but formidable land predator.

It was now fully time to start my return home. Whether to go while the duende was close but occupied by hornets or to wait on the chance that it was moving clear away was a toss-up. I decided to go.

The edge of the swamp, the bamboos and the close

thicket behind them were hard on the nerves. I could see nothing. The rifle was so useless that I was tempted to sling it and trust to the machete to deal with any sudden attack; but of course I could not bring myself to do so. I examined every clump before passing it and tried always to face the long grass and looser undergrowth in which an animal could hide, and to keep at my back the impenetrable stuff from which a charge was unlikely.

This meant a wretchedly slow journey. I did not want to climb to the ridge again, where the going would be slower still, so when I came to the beginning of my own path to the water I cut my way straight on. At last I came out into the big timber at the foot of the ridge and felt more confident, though the trees were set too close together for my liking.

When I had covered rather more than a mile — it is difficult to be exact about distance unless one can see well ahead — I turned north and made straight for the long glade. This sudden turn is interesting. I can remember no reason whatever for my decision. I knew where I was. I knew that by making for the glade I should add to my journey. Yet the change of direction was sharp, imperative, unarguable.

In another ten minutes or so I began to run. I did not even make any determined effort to stop myself; the most that my superior human brain could do for me was to insist that I go straight. Even that was difficult. The hair on the back of my neck was bristling. I was panting. I was inclined to run into obstructions or to

[189]

lose direction when I went round them. The circling must have partly begun, for when I trotted into the long glade I was closer to the cliff than to the middle. It was perhaps as well. I could burst out into the sun with hardly any delay.

Open space reminded me that I had once claimed to be salted against peccary panic. Thirty yards out from the edge of the glade I dropped to the ground under cover of dead tufts of grass and turned round to face the forest. I was having no more nonsense about rare animals. If I saw what I was dead certain I was going to see, I meant to kill.

Twenty seconds later the mustelid appeared low down in the ferns. It was not much of a target and I should not have spotted it at all if I had not been concentrating on my own track. I fired and was sure that I had put the bullet behind the right shoulder — a shot which should have raked the lungs on its way to more damage; but when I got up and walked to the spot — the smell of cordite having restored my courage like a tot of rum — there was no sign of blood, only a powerful patch of scent. At least I had now handed out some alarm myself. I had no intention of being a proper sahib and following my wounded beast into the jungle — the main object being, I gather, to prevent disablement turning it into a man-eater. That seemed unnecessary when all the evidence suggested that the duende found human flesh as edible as any other.

This has taught me a lot more of its habits. First: it

is a forest dweller which does not kill in the open except at night; it was hot on my trail but obviously hesitated to enter the glade. Second: it does not stalk its prey. Joaquín said as much after examining the print which he thought might be of otter. The movement of the bamboos by the swamp and the swaying of fern tops prove that it is an inefficient stalker. Game would be alerted and away like a shot. The mustelid chases, not very fast but relentlessly.

It may also lie up in ambush after foreseeing by instinct or experience, like any other carnivore, the probable track of the oncoming game. That is what I think happened. My change of direction was a wholly unconscious warning — very difficult to be understood by any townsman with all his natural instincts degenerated — that if I walked straight on I should run into certain trouble.

I am becoming a connoisseur and analyst of fear. There is a definite distinction between that unconscious warning and the Declaration of Intent; the latter produces a conscious terror in every way equivalent to that caused by the classical ghost, whether or not the ghost is an illusion.

It may be that the fear is the reality, which itself causes the illusion, rather than the other way round. I am reminded of: *And turns no more his head because he knows a frightful fiend doth close behind him tread.* Coleridge must have guessed that by instinct. It's a fact. One runs and does not turn one's head. Or would not turn it if one hadn't a rifle. But I have still to clarify my thinking on this whole subject. It is difficult without a library; and even among books one would probably be muddled by the psychologists who invent one phobia after another but don't know the first damned thing about real, justified, animal fear.

To return to the journey. All of it must be recorded for future reference. My mind is inclined to suppress and forget incidents which are disgraceful or temporarily unacceptable. If I had not been able to look up what I wrote on May 3, I should have sublimated the memory and been unable to compare my two experiences of sheer cowardice or to draw conclusions from them.

I trotted down the long glade — making up time, not running away — and headed straight for the point of easiest access to the forest where any game in a hurry would crash through into the trees. I hoped the duende was dead or dying but, if it wasn't, that was where it would wait for me.

I could not tell how good its long sight was. Available evidence suggested that the round eyes were as good as a cat's in darkness but not designed for daylight. So I dropped down, vanished into the grass again and crawled off to the southeast at right angles to my former course. I had not far to go before I could safely stand up. Then I skirted the well glade, and just in time picked up the cathedral aisle. The light was beginning to fail and the racket in the treetops was at full blast. The duende certainly could not hear my progress any more than I could hear his. I reckoned that I was quite safe, always provided that I could reach the llano before dark, for the timber was so well spaced that I had time to use the rifle and space to swing it. I did consider spending the night in a tree on the rare occasions when I saw one that was climbable, but the thought of Chucha's anxiety was just enough to prevent it.

I longed for a horse, especially Tesoro, who would have used his gift for dodging fast through woodland to get us out of there in ten minutes. As it was, ten minutes merely brought deeper dusk and slower progress. The just visible compass gave me direction but could not tell me where the passage was. It was really my little howling cousins, the monkeys, who led me out. They were holding a students' demonstration at their usual playground on the edge of the llano, and ears were a quicker guide to it than eyes. I marched on straight for the excitement, when a little casting about revealed starshine and the gap.

I thought that somewhere I heard the slow beat of horses' hooves and supposed they had broken away through the open gate while Mario was moving them from the corral to the hall. I cursed his carelessness, for the llano in darkness so close to the forest could be thoroughly dangerous. I did not much care for it myself in spite of the stars. Then I heard Chucha's voice calling for Ojen and I let out a yell in answer. She was up in a moment, riding Pichón and leading Tesoro — which always takes some doing. When dusk fell and still I was not home, she had forced Mario to help her to saddle up, choosing Tesoro because of her belief that he looks after me, and ridden straight across the creek and down to the gap. Courage beyond belief! I wonder if she would be proof against the Declaration of Intent. Perhaps. I know that I should be if I thought her in danger. But I have a rifle, and she has nothing much but an amateur *chiripá*. However, she must never do this again.

[*May 10, Tuesday*]

The scent of her body reminds me of that other. One would think that by association I ought to find it repulsive. Far from it! Many lovers must know what I mean. Our own females also possess a musk gland — unless the whole thing is an illusion and comparable to the sweet odors recorded by saints and mystics. It is emitted in moments of profound and passionate emotion and has nothing whatever to do with perfume or the normal excretions of the female.

Life and death combine in that supersensual fragrance, for in the act of creation I sometimes think that we ought, like the male spider, to die. And what is death itself but coalescence with the unknown?

So much for the intrusion into my bed of unity with my fellow animals! A more unpleasant unity was very close yesterday. This morning, now knowing what to look for, I found clear tracks in the adobe dust beneath the wall where Mario had built it up. The pair followed us home.

[*May 11, Wednesday*]

They have got Tesoro. Why did I ever come here? Why don't I get out now? This is intolerable. I wish I had some man of my own kind to talk to — Valera, the two guerrilleros, anybody. I cannot make up my mind. I am neither a zoologist nor a sportsman nor any kind of blasted hero. I have been a fool not to tell Mario and Chucha the truth and I cannot do so now. At least I think I can't. It is better that they should go on believing in dwarfs and keep everything shut at night until the rains come and cut these slender devils off from the llano for another twelve years or more. What is my duty? Have I any duty? I must not clear out till I have persuaded Mario and Teresa to settle in Santa Eulalia. They won't, I know.

We may now be left in peace. What is certain is that this present generation of mustelids is keenly aware of a new source of food. The drought brought them over the creek for the first time. They then learned that horses were harmless and that men ran as well as peccary and deer. I am now sure that at first I was to them an animal of their own kind and therefore had to be cautiously observed before it was classed irrevocably as game. Remembering the musk and the plunging of Tesoro, it is clear to me that on the occasion of our first visit to the ridge we were watched but allowed to go.

This morning I had no intention of collecting muste-lids. I wanted to give Tesoro some needed exercise and to clear up my own mind which had been forced by more than duendes into too much introspection, too many impossible designs for our future. Valera and the guerrilleros could not help in that personal problem, unless it would do me good to be laughed at. I told Chu-cha quite truthfully that I was not going to enter the forest and that I intended to ride fast as far south as I could go — a distance which would be beyond her and make her painfully saddlesore. We might, I said, take out Pichón and Estrellera in the evening.

I carried the 16-bore in the saddle holster with the usual No. 5 cartridges in my belt and a few No. 2's in my pocket. I also took a grain feed for Tesoro and a good lunch for myself since this was a sort of holiday outing in spirit. We crossed the creek and cantered along it until the tall timber began to close the horizon and the forest swung to the east to form a deep, dense belt along the Guaviare. I had not been down at the bot-tom of the funnel, where the creek enters the trees, since early days at the estancia. I was then considering a canoe with an outboard motor and direct communica-tion with the Guaviare. It was out of the question. The creek was not navigable — a wild wilderness of fallen trees, swamps and floating grasses.

There were a few stagnant pools on our route which became more frequent as we approached the Guaviare forest belt. I looked in the mud for tracks and found them. A duende had stopped to drink. Further upstream, the estancia is, I think, the extreme limit of their range; if it were not for the horses, they would never go so far from the forest. But down there to the south they could leave the trees, cross the dry creek and slink back into cover. They could then approach Santa Eulalia without ever taking to open llano at all. They may have done so in some long forgotten drought. What it was that danced (when a guitar was playing?) remained a rumor in the grass. Even in settled territory a nocturnal animal is rarely seen. Here where rivers are the only roads and the forest is neither explored nor worth exploring there is not even anyone to see it.

The country was thickish parkland — say, three or four trees to the acre, all noticeably suffering from drought. Even a single horseman left behind eddies of powdery soil hanging in the windless air. I should say that in the unending war between trees and grassland the forest had recently advanced and was now in course of being thrown back from occupied territory. After the rains this no-man's-land had been an Eden of astonishing beauty, part sun, part shade, with game always to be seen. Yesterday it was almost leafless, for our only winter is the winter of drought.

Tesoro was at his most affectionate. He was determined to eat my lunch as well as his own and snorted with disgust at the smell of animal fat when he found that Teresa's appetizing crusts hid half a pullet. He had

was too long a dispute between us. All the while I kept as sharp a lookout to the west as he allowed. I did not want to turn my back on the thickening forest and edged away towards the bed of the creek. The wind veered again to the south. He was then sweating and unhappy but quite amenable. I hoped that the scent he had picked up was jaguar. I was pretty sure it was not.

We were nearing the open parkland and in ten minutes more would have been a mere point in the empty semicircle of the llano when again he bolted. His skill among trees seemed to have deserted him. A low branch which his head had only just cleared nearly had me off. Just as soon as I had taken my face out of his mane he was into another. Fortunately for me it was only an overhanging mass of twigs, but it was solid enough to sweep me out of the saddle and leave me clinging and struggling to disentangle myself.

Tesoro was still going at full gallop through the tall timber and bearing far too much to the right. I ran after him but it was hopeless. Though the trees were well spaced, visibility at best was limited to quarter of a mile.

The mustelid passed quite close, loping along with its leisurely, high-arched canter. It must have seen me but paid no attention at all. I was not chosen. I was like the herd of peccary which had left an open space. It seemed to be picking up the scent at the end of each leap. The nose close to the ground exaggerated the looping effect. It had of course nothing like the speed of Tesoro, but kept steadily on until it too vanished among trees.

I shouted to Tesoro aloud to run to the llano, for God's sake straight to the llano, hardly realizing what I was doing until I became conscious of the hoarseness of my throat. Wherever he had gone, it was far away, for there was no sound anywhere except the scraping of dry leaves in the light breeze.

I climbed a tree in the hope of seeing him, but found that I had a longer view on the ground. When I came down again I heard the drum of his hooves approaching and ran towards him, trying to keep my voice calm as well as loud. He passed across my front a hundred yards away, curving towards the gloom, the gold of his coat darkened by sweat and streaked with foam, the gun in its holster bouncing against his flank. He did not turn, never heard or saw me probably. He was near the end of his endurance. The mustelid appeared on his trail two or three minutes later, unhurried, still loping effortlessly along.

I never expected to see Tesoro again, but I underrated the utter cruelty, the hypnosis of the Declaration of Intent. He passed out of sight and hearing but it was not long before again I glimpsed what was left of his gold dodging through the black trunks. He was going at a slow canter now. Once he pecked and was down on his knees, then off again using the last of his breath for a despairing neigh. This second circle in which he ran was so much smaller than the first that I raced frantically across the diagonal in the hope of intercepting him. It could not be done. I only got near enough to be in at the death.

The mustelid bounded into sight ten lengths behind him, never quickening pace, trusting to the exhaustion and terror of the prey. The final attack was a short spurt and a tremendous leap which landed it on Tesoro's back. It bit him straight through the axis, twisting its head to bring the fangs to bear on each side of the spine, and Tesoro went down head over heels, the mustelid jumping clear and then slinking to the throat which it tore open.

Its eyes were just above the level of Tesoro's prostrate neck and closed in ecstasy as it lapped. When it opened them it saw me. There was no handy tree, and even if there had been I do not think I would have turned my back when two long springs could reach me. It crouched down with forepaws on Tesoro. Face and whiskers were dabbled with blood which dripped from the points of the white, bared canines.

I was not prey. I was a creature, like the jaguar, which had dared to interfere with a meal. I expected a fierce but harmless demonstration warning me to clear off or to be killed; but there was none. It meant business from the start, crawling towards me with belly nearly touching the ground. It looked more like some kind of thick, furry snake than a mammal.

I could only stand my ground and hope that the shining machete would be taken as my own demonstration

— a better proof than growls and open mouth that I too meant business. I remember thinking that I was the heavier of the two beasts and that cold steel was better than teeth. I felt anger rather than fear. Adrenalin and high blood pressure, I suppose. My life force was aware that fear could not save it.

There must have been some transference, for the mustelid hesitated. It probably did not care for a frontal attack, which was unfamiliar; its prey always turned tail. Hesitation was very short. Like all its kin, even those which are not aggressive, its courage was without limits. The challenger might be behaving in a manner outside its experience, but the end would be that which always happened.

A full spring must have had me down, but it came on with leisurely crawl till it was not more than two yards from me. When it exposed its throat and before it could get fairly launched I lunged forward. The point of the machete, too wide for an effective stab, got caught in the loose, tough skin, pushing a thick fold of it sideways. The force with which we met was enough to roll both of us over. Any feline could then have finished me with a stroke of the paw, but the mustelid had to get its jaws to bear. As it turned head and shoulders I struck out backhanded with the machete and slammed it full on the nose. To my amazement it toppled over as suddenly as Tesoro. I ran to the saddle holster, recovered the gun and blew the back of its head in just as it was getting up from the count.

How long did this take from the time the beast looked over the neck and saw me? I simply do not know. Seconds, not minutes. One's own body clock is speeded up so fast that it is impossible to tell. I am sure that the elapsed time was much less than I felt it to be because the other mustelid who must have taken part in the hunting—not chasing but moving position, I believe, to reinforce panic by a whiff of scent — had only just come to the kill.

I saw her dancing behind a cactus to sum up the unprecedented situation. That gave me time to slip a No. 2 cartridge into the choke barrel. She charged directly from her cover and I took her on the second bound at something less than eight yards. I could see that the right ear was perforated and partly torn away from the head; but the main blast of heavy shot which must have hit her between the eyes seemed to have little effect except that she turned and ran. Evidently courage was not quite unlimited. I was right in predicting the strength of the frontal bone of the skull.

It was the male which I had stunned with the machete. Hornets could have done it no harm except on that vulnerable nose and the corners of the mouth where there was an exposed bit of hairless lower lip — possibly an individual deformity, possibly connected with the sockets in which the long fangs fitted while at rest.

I started to skin it, but found the tough hide defeated an amateur. I was also exhausted, impatient and had

copiously shat myself. Cleaning up, sobbing over Tesoro and pulling the machete in and out of its sheath
seemed occupation enough. I am inefficient at both
cleaning and skinning. Mario deals with any game
which I bring home.

The mustelid was smaller and lighter than I had
thought, weighing perhaps a hundred and twenty
pounds, less rather than more. Its true size was exaggerated by the length of the body when fully extended
and the loose skin when relaxed. All the other dwarf
legends could be as true as that of the dance. Claws
were weak. Though the beast could jump to a considerable height, it could not hang on, let alone climb. That
it could not swim also seemed possible; it might well
have difficulty in keeping the heavy skull above water.
But I am too ignorant of comparative anatomy to be
sure. An alternative explanation could be that on land
this mustelid has no experience of enemies. Even the
jaguar, though dead certain to be the winner if not dis-
abled, feels the "superstitious" fear and does not stop to
argue. Alligators, however, could deal very easily with
that slender body, and on the edge of the water ray and
electric eel would be more dangerous still.

I confirmed that my shot from the long glade had hit
exactly where I thought it did; but there was no shoulder in the way, not even flesh, only the badly fitting
overcoat of the crouching animal. The dumdum might
as well have hit a sandbag. I found a neat point of
entry. The bullet had then passed under the belly and

out, leaving a ragged wound which did not appear to have bled much or to have caused the beast any inconvenience.

The carcass was of course too heavy to carry, so I covered it with brushwood and left it. Tesoro's saddle and tack I piled at some distance from his body to avoid damage by the vultures. He too seemed very small in death. I have noticed that before, when my first ponies in Argentina died, though never with such love and pity. How do they carry us so easily and gallantly while life is still in them?

The walk home tired and exasperated me more than any of distances I had covered going to and from the ridge. If I kept to the cool darkness I was continually zigzagging through trees; if I took to the open llano I was baked by that intolerable ball of fire. No wonder the llaneros never dismount! All the way there was something bothering memory, connected with my observations of this unique mustelid; yet I could not pull it up to the surface.

It was simply a difference of size which was preventing instant association. I got at it by way of the badger. I had not missed the parallel of the tremendous jaw, the supporting crest of bone and the vulnerable nose. The badger took me back to cold, green England: to Rendcomb where their habits have been closely studied and thus to Rendcomb Agricultural College where I was invited to give a couple of lectures on soil survey in the tropics. In the senior common room after dinner I settled down with a zoologist whose name I forget. He was an authority on small mammals, particularly European mammals, and he gave it as his opinion that of all the carnivores — with the possible exception of man — the most courageous, the most savage, the most tenacious in the chase was the stoat; and like the weasel and the polecat it killed for the sake of killing.

He was full of stories of the stoat. Cornered, it would unhesitatingly attack and spring to the height of the waist. One would be wise to grab it quickly off one's coat, at the expense of a badly bitten hand, before it reached the throat. He was doubtful if it ever hunted in pack — the smaller weasel undoubtedly did — but farm hands and even reliable gamekeepers had stories of meeting half a dozen stoats in sunk lanes or on woodland paths and getting out of there quick with the little bodies — another point of resemblance — looping along behind.

Both stoat and weasel live in thick cover and use it cunningly. They come out only to hunt or for curiosity. To satisfy curiosity they all sit up to see over obstacles. They kill by seizing the prey at the back of the skull, the teeth penetrating the brain.

This mustelid appears to be on the least specialized line of descent, from which the badgers and the otters have branched off. I wish I knew whether the stoat also hunts downwind. I believe the lion is the only carnivore which does. One animal gives its scent and so drives the prey straight into an ambush laid by another. The killing of Tesoro shows that the mustelids use this trick, but with an important difference. The prey is selected and then relentlessly followed till it drops. The second animal, if not chasing, moves about and gives its scent from various angles to reinforce panic and to ensure that the game does not run straight.

Scent, however, is only an auxiliary. When the wind veered to the west and Tesoro bolted, I am certain there was no mustelid to the east to send him off in a circle. For one thing, the country was becoming too open for them in daylight; for another the wind was too changeable for any planning. Tesoro could have bolted for the llano. He did not. I could have taken the line I knew in the forest. I did not. No, there is more to it than scent. One must also remember that in thick forest there is rarely any wind at all.

This singling out of the chosen quarry, the refusal to go off on the trail of any other and the uncontrollable panic of the hunted together add up to what I have called the Declaration of Intent. It is possible that the musk glands release molecules which act directly on the nervous system. That sounds decently material and scientific, but begs too many questions. A more promising line of investigation is the "superstitious" fear. I have experienced it. I know how it inhibits the inborn mechanism of self-preservation as well as the sense of direction. At that level of consciousness I am not an expert in tropical agriculture; I am a hunted mammal.

The rabbit resembles me sufficiently for it to be a

primitive working model in the laboratories. The rabbit which the stoat selects runs straight to start with, then in a circle. Finally it squats down and squeals. Whether it takes to burrow or cover or the open it cannot escape and gives the impression of knowing it. Only long observation of this Colombian mustelid and its tiny relatives could confirm my tentative theory: that a certain quality of fear can operate at a distance, and that this enables the mustelid to hunt in the way it does.

That brought me, while I plodded on through the heat, to the question: what *is* fear? It is not fear of death. The rabbit and Tesoro can have no knowledge of death. Fear is nothing but a chemical change in the organism directed towards keeping itself in a fit state to breed other organisms. But that may be putting the cart before the horse. The adrenalin is secreted after the fear. Leave it at this — fear is an unreasoning, instinctive order to run.

Panic so overwhelming that the animal does not run but sits trembling and takes what is coming is as familiar to man as the rabbit. He cowers before the man-eater, the earthquake and unendurable shelling. Although so powerful, ingenious and bloodthirsty an ape is never helpless, the instincts of self-preservation are inhibited. He sits. He turns no more his head. He pulls the blanket over it.

Somewhere there is the key to the behavior of stoat and rabbit. I still think the adjective "superstitious" helps. Fear of the unseen is the most inhibiting of all.

But how are we aware of the unseen, unheard, unscented? Pure imagination. I disagree, but accept it for the sake of argument with myself. However it gets us no farther towards knowledge of the receiving mechanism.

I got in, dead tired, just before dusk. Chucha rode down the creek to meet me, leading Estrellera. She said that she knew I needed another horse to carry a deer. A rationalization of her awareness that I did indeed want a horse. How close we are!

I told her that Tesoro had been killed by a puma, that I had shot it but too late. Somehow I had to account for my distress. She cried, Indians are very fond of pets, and to her Tesoro was the prize pet. Then she comforted me like — like what? A dear daughter, perhaps, who understands every elemental emotion and does not look beyond.

[*Evening*]

She set her heart on coming with me to see Tesoro, and I could not refuse. I felt reasonably sure that the wounded mustelid would have deserted the open woodland and taken refuge in deep cover. So I mounted her on Estrellera and myself rode the broader Pichón. He's a good, solid, old stick, but he too tried to tear down the corral.

Since I had got up early this morning, urgently written up the record of yesterday, and then dozed off, it was nearly eleven when we started instead of the regulation hour of six. I badly wanted the skin or at least the head of the mustelid intact, but it couldn't be helped. I haven't a bloody great gang of coolies to carve up my specimen, preserving the bones for a museum and the hide for my living room — where the lizards, the rats and the ants would get it however much Mario and I salted it. In the rainy season I should probably find a couple of trees growing through it as well.

As we rode south, much more slowly than yesterday, Chucha began to search for the truth of my daylong absences. At home she was too dutiful to reveal her fears, but now we were on a joint expedition and bound together by sorrow for Tesoro. Dutiful. Well, not quite that. She is so free to ask questions and be answered that she lays off the subjects such as our future and dwarf-hunting which are exclusive to me. Tactful, perhaps. Or is she afraid of the answers?

"You are always thinking of them, Ojen," she said.

"It could be that there are five minutes in the day when I do not think of you."

"Last night in your sleep you were calling for your machete. I got up and gave it to you, but your hand did not want it."

"I suppose I had cut down what I was dreaming about."

"Did they kill Tesoro? You must swear to me."

"I swear to you that a beast killed Tesoro. You will see it."

I hoped to be able to pass off the mustelid as a puma, though it was remarkably uncatlike except for the fangs. After all, she had never seen a puma, wild or in a zoo, and Indian legend makes it a far more formidable animal than it really is.

I need not have been anxious. When we arrived, the vultures were competing with the ants. Tesoro was a red ruin. Chucha still wanted to touch him but I would not let her. There was such a phalanx of red predator ants spread over him that the exposed muscles of loins and back seemed to be moving. If she went too close the little devils would be all over her arms and legs in a second.

The ants had not found the other carcass, but the birds had. When I came up, two tayras who had been making a meal of their larger cousin gave me a dirty look and slowly removed themselves. They are omnivorous and harmless and have the same air of independence as the badger. They had scratched away my covering of brushwood and let in the vultures.

The mustelid was much the worse for wear and could pass as a light-colored puma. Even so Chucha was puzzled. She thought that a puma had longer legs, she said, and she was sure that it had a longer tail. I replied that my first shot had hit the tail and cut it off. An incredibly unlikely fluke, but a good enough story for anyone who had never handled a gun. What was left of the tip of the tail was red and raw.

There was no trophy, nothing worth carrying home

except Tesoro's saddle and tack. We rode back lazily, keeping to the scattered shade on the edge of the llano while Chucha babbled happily but not altogether at random. She managed to bring the conversation back to dwarfs again.

What islands we are! I doubt if any woman understands the deep loneliness to which men condemn themselves. They think it a moroseness and that our silence in some way disparages them as inferior creatures. We are merely away. The business of the island is briskly proceeding, but all around it is sea and no boat. Women cannot ever accept that there is no boat. Chucha does accept it as a rule, thereby making our relations so deliciously easy.

"Ojen, have you talked to the dwarfs yet?"

"Not yet."

"Are they afraid of you?"

"Probably."

She thought over that unsatisfactory answer and then asked me what weapons they had.

"Only magic."

"What can they do?"

"Nothing, if one feels no fear."

"They will never work for you," she said. "The rains are coming and we shall all be busy again. We do not need them, Ojen, so let us leave them alone."

It was the first time I ever heard her use that proprietary "we." I love the confidence it shows. Which of us am I going to betray?

I agreed to leave them alone and I shall keep my word. Now that I know what it is that dances, there is no more point in exposing myself on that abominable ridge. If the remaining mustelid recovers, the flowing creek will limit its movements. I have read somewhere that it takes a thousand years to establish an instinctive fear of man, but I think the lesson should be sufficient to instill caution, so long as there are enough peccary and tapir on its home ground to satisfy the hunger of a duende.

This evening clouds are drifting past the moon for the first time since early December.

[*May 14, Saturday*]

Sun again. One greets it as an old friend whose energy is intolerable but whose absence leaves one irresolute. The first great blobs of rain splashed down at dawn yesterday, puffing the dust like charges of shot. One solid silver-edged cloud was being chased to the northwest by the main fleet, with only two hand's breadths of blue sky between them. Then our closed, black world boiled over and rolled with thunder, hit after hit landing on the infinite target of the llano and one on the main building, which fortunately did no damage.

A terrifying storm. I expected a more gradual onslaught of the rains. We have had nine inches in twenty-four hours. At one time the garden was a lake between walls and we all paddled about trying to close the inlets of the irrigation channels.

The marshes overflowed suddenly when the natural dam of mud and decayed vegetation disintegrated. I was in time to see the bore, three or four feet high, tear up the underlying silt and go roaring down the bed of the creek at the speed of a galloping horse — a tremendous skewbald of brown and white. Behind it the creek spread out till it was nearly up to the rubbish dump, and I began to wonder what we should use for a boat if the stream reached the estancia. It didn't. It settled into a great river half the size of the Guaviare and is now going down, leaving behind a band of alluvium where in three days I shall see a flicker of green and in a week a carpet of grass as thick as English turf.

Our adobe walls have collapsed in a dozen places and would not keep out an agouti, let alone duendes. But the mustelids will never visit us again, assuming that such a drought as this occurs only once in a dozen or more years. Then their cubs might. But, walls or no walls, the experimental station will be secure so long as my successors — if there are any — keep up the rules which Mario has always obeyed and never understood. How right he was never to cross the garden at night and to see that windows were barred or shuttered, and all doors locked!

I have a new Chucha. She has done her best to be a Child of the Sun, but I suspect she is more at ease in the downpour of the Upper Amazon where she was brought up, and takes it for granted that human beings should live in a hot bath, decently wet between the blasts of sunshine. Indecently wet would be more like it. She ought to go stark naked. Her combination of one provocative, soaked garment and pathetic drowned-kitten relaxation invites immediate attention. I noticed that even old Mario was affected. So did Teresa — and told him to come in and mend the roof.

At the same time Chucha has developed a wild gaiety. She reminds me of a child on its first visit to the seaside. Bucket and spade and impulsive kisses. It could be that she feels not only the joy of the rains but also the glorious freedom of her lover from all these weeks of idiocy. My job is to make a ton of wheat grow where now there is only one palatable tuft of grass for a bullock, not to dispute the forest with animals to which the Lord gave such outstanding power and beauty — though I can't say as much for their habits.

Somehow one expects the sun to be less fiery after the rain, but of course it is not. The llano steams. Chucha's garment dries to comparative respectability in twenty minutes. The mud crusts very quickly and can be treacherous as thin ice. I must ride up and see how far the marshes now extend to the north and what temporary streams are running into them. Seen from the Mother and Child I expect to find the llano all striped with blue and silver, for the water level must be too high to be hidden by the shallow folds.

The floods will soon go down and then be stationary

[215]

for four months, fed by daily rains. I ought to make a swimming pool for Chucha on one of the minor soak-aways of the marsh. Or it could easily be done by damming the creek when the level is stabilized. Now, how on earth could I have written that? Proof of how swiftly one can throw off an obsession when the environment changes! To dam the creek is something which never must be allowed.

[*May 15, Sunday*]

It is time the Government replaced Pedro. The Intendencia must know by now that he has vanished and ought to have sent someone along who could take my evidence. But, to be fair, why should they give a damn for a back end of beyond with ownerless cattle and ownerless men? Apart from the incalculable results of rotgut working on a horseman's pride — much as it did in sixteenth-century Europe — our life is peaceful, hostility between human beings being pointless when we are all isolated in a hostile environment. The Intendencia knows very well that we govern ourselves by mutual consent with a minimum of murder, and that any emergency will have settled itself long before uniforms and the law arrive.

Chucha and I set out early and rode up the east side of the marshes. The ground was too soft for her to come to any harm, so I let her have her first all-out gallop.

Estrellera easily beat Pichón over five furlongs and showed a ladylike pride. Chucha, the darling, was ecstatic.

The marshes have not broadened as much as I expected, but the water has inundated three or four miles along the line of a slight depression which was hardly perceptible in the drought. From the Mother and Child we saw four llaneros riding round the head of the flood, their course marked by white flecks of water from the pools instead of eddies of dust. As soon as they sighted us, they galloped towards us. They were Alvar, Arnoldo — in his capacity of temporary headman — a fellow called Vicente who was a particular friend of Pedro's and a fourth who rides the country far beyond Santa Eulalia and is only known to me by sight.

They greeted us with proper solemnity and were particularly formal with Chucha who has acquired my social status. These indispensable ceremonies over, they were eager to know if I had seen any other riders and burst into their story. Vicente told it; Arnoldo threw in a few proverbs from time to time; and Alvar cursed.

On Friday morning at the height of the storm three guerrilleros in the usual jeep, bristling with arms, had splashed into Santa Eulalia and taken refuge under the first solid thatch they came to. The men were all out on the llano, weather or no weather, riding round the frightened herds, and there was hardly anybody in the settlement but the women and Arnoldo. Arnoldo made the unwelcome visitors as comfortable as he could and continued his work — a marked discourtesy — pretending that he did not know who they were.

When the men and horses, sodden and cold, began to drift in at dusk, they did not dismount and surrounded the jeep. I suppose there were about a dozen of them, upright in the saddle, patient as Indians, watching with the veiled eyes of ceremonious killers. The partisans demanded cattle. According to Vicente, none of the llaneros had replied, either refusing or accepting. It must have been obvious to the jeep party that these were men of a different breed from their submissive mountain peasants, and that bloodshed meant nothing to them.

The guerrilleros quickly regained the jeep. With all that firepower concentrated on their semicircle, the llaneros had at least to produce some words. They agreed to drive another bunch of cattle to the foothills of the Cordillera, though they had no intention whatever of doing so. Machine-gunning from the air had put more fear of God and the Government into them than a hundred men on the ground.

Moreover, Alvar said, these fatherless bandits were men of education, well spoken. That puzzled him. It doesn't puzzle me. The bastards, as he rightly called them, are enjoying themselves. They think the eyes of history are on them. Many are law students or unemployable lawyers; so they like playing at soldiers. I hope to live to see the day when soldiers like playing at being lawyers.

They must have eaten the villages out of house and home and become very short of rations, for they were taking big risks besides gambling against the meteorological reports. They may have thought that open llano was always open llano and they could of course be confident — after their punitive expeditions against remote villages in the Cordillera — that knives and the odd lance were not much use against machine pistols.

They dossed down, two sleeping and one on guard, in front of the ashes of Pedro's place — a position from which they could cover all four tracks of Santa Eulalia. At dawn on Saturday there was still no sign of a break in the downpour, and it looked as if the whole settlement was about to slide down the gentle slope into the Guaviare. They were in a filthy temper and decided to get out quick. They swore to return and burn the place down if the cattle were not delivered on time.

Two miles out they tried to ford a yellow torrent and stuck fast. They hauled out the jeep backwards, found a likelier crossing and stuck again. God wished the jeep to remain there, Arnoldo said, and remain there it did. All that could be seen of it was one wheel cocked up in a slope of mud.

But God had failed to foresee the consequences. The three, furious and with mud running off them in streams, had marched back and demanded horses. This would have been perfectly acceptable in any large estancia, but not in Santa Eulalia where a man had no possessions but his horse and saddle. Cattle, all right.

Women, well, there might be one or two who would consider it an honor. But horses, no!

They took what they wanted, three horses and three remounts. It turned out that they actually needed less, for their leader was neatly spitted on a long lance. The gallant llanero at the butt end was turned into a fountain. They wrote a cross on him with their guns, Alvar said. After that, resistance was hopeless.

The sun was now out again and steaming the mud. The guerrilleros coolly dried themselves, commandeered what food they could lay their hands on and rode off leading their two spare horses in the late afternoon. Before dusk five llaneros followed hard on their tracks, careful to stay out of sight. They hoped to be able to close in with the twilight when their steel would have a chance against automatic weapons. Alternative tactics would be to creep up when the two men camped for the night, cut the horses loose and round them up at leisure. A number of unpleasant things could happen to the pursued if they had to make their way back to the Cordillera on foot.

The two guerrilleros followed the forest belt along the Guaviare. Since the more open space they had for their weapons, the more unassailable they would be, this route was unexpected. The llaneros, cleverly using the folds and skylines which only they could recognize, watched them unsaddle and tether the horses. When darkness came down, they closed in on foot. They found the temporary camp all right, and nothing on the ground but horse dung.

They were innocent, of course. They seemed to have assumed that no men were as valiant and cunning as themselves. They did not realize that these veterans, though knowing comparatively little of horses and the lay of the land, had been hunted for years by experienced, well-armed enemies and were fully capable of foreseeing what the llaneros were likely to do before the honest souls thought of it themselves.

The pursuers had wasted a lot of time but still had a trick in hand. Hoofprints were distinguished with fingers and matches and established that the four horses had quietly moved on westwards. That meant that sooner or later the guerrilleros would be stopped by the lower reaches of the creek. They could not possibly cross it, so they would have to follow it up and go round the north of the marshes.

Four of the llaneros then struck straight across the grass through the night in order to intercept them. The fifth stayed on the edge of the forest as his horse was finished. A shameful failure in their ordinary daily life. Their horses, though they always look thin and ungroomed and are often saddlesore, can endure anything. But this one, which its owner had had to grab in a hurry, had been weakened by a vampire bat the night before.

The four, when we met them, had found no hoof-

prints north of the marsh and were sure that the guerrilleros were still in the Guaviare forest belt. I said that
I doubted it. They knew of the existence of creek and
marshes as well as the llaneros did. If they wanted to
break contact, they could have followed the forest for a
mile or two and then ridden off into the blue. It did not
much matter where they found themselves at sunrise.
They had only to put it at their backs and go on.

Alvar, who had lost his own reliable mount to them,
would not have it. If they had got that far ahead they
would kill their horses, he said furiously, at the pace
they were going. I don't suppose they cared. Assuming
their jeep was the same as I saw at the estancia, it had a
two-way radio in it. Before they abandoned the vehicle
they could have called up guerrilla headquarters and
reported their intention. Thus, if they could only keep
their lead for another day, a party might come out to
pick them up.

The four swept off their hats, thanking us for our
sympathy and help — though we could give none —
and paced on to the west.

Chucha has revised her opinion of revolutionaries.
Why do idealists have to kill people, she wants to know.
I forget the exact words she used. Idealist is not in her
vocabularly. It is extraordinary how we can communicate in depth on any subject, even mildly technical subjects, with language which is really only fit to ask for a
banana.

[*May 16, Monday*]

We tried to plow too soon and broke a tine of the cultivator on new ground outside the walls. The water had poured off, soaking in a mere three inches and leaving the soil rock hard beneath. I must remember that if I am here next year.

If I am here. I long to be. That would solve so many problems. But it is highly improbable. Both my director and the Government, when they know everything, will insist that this is a lunatic choice for an experimental station. If only I had someone to talk to! This goes round and round in circles. I am obsessed with Chucha. It isn't only our exquisite incontinence. I swear I should still cherish her simplicity and grace and youth if she or I were impotent. There is only one word to describe what I feel for her, and I cannot and will not face it.

Oh God! Back to broken ironmongery and mustelids. They may settle the issue yet.

I rode into Santa Eulalia with the two halves of the tine knowing that if Arnoldo had them for a model he could laboriously forge another. I found the men, dark-faced, standing by their horses in the plaza. They told me there had been another murder by the partisans, who had brutally cut the throat of that unfortunate llanero left behind with his exhausted horse.

The other four had returned home early this morning, having given up the chase as hopeless. They found that their companion — Jacinto, his name was — had not come in, though he could easily have walked the distance in three hours. They rode out to meet him, and caught his hobbled horse far out on the llano. Jacinto was where they had left him, lying on a bed of dry leaves with his throat cut.

I had to go to his house, view the body they had brought in and speak the nothings of convention to his weeping Indian wife. What happens to the widows? Where do they go and how do they live? I glanced at the unpleasant sight and then looked more carefully. I asked Alvar — sure to be experienced in such matters — whether he had seen many men before with gaping throats.

"Two, or it could be three. It is not," he added apologetically, "a very rare occurrence."

"Didn't the killer usually do a neater job?"

"I believe it! But what can you expect of these sons of whores? They cannot even handle a knife like a gentleman."

"Was there much blood?"

"It seemed to me little. But leaves are more thirsty than the ground. And there had been rain in the night."

I embarked cautiously on the forbidden subject.

"Have you always grazed cattle along the belt of the Guaviare?"

"Without a care!"

"Jaguar?"

"None! There is no game left for them to eat. We had

not always such a lack of powder and shot as there is now."

"Could there be other hunters?"

"Not a thought! You know where those live better than any of us."

I asked him what tracks they had seen. Unfortunately they had taken murder for granted and had pretty well ignored tracks. Jacinto had been sleeping just inside a grove of ceibas, on the same spot where the two fugitives with their four horses had pretended to be about to camp. Naturally there were prints of feet and hooves all over the place. It was difficult to judge which had been made before the killing and which afterwards, especially as there had been a short, violent storm in the night, turning the grove into an island. What was clear was the indentation of two knees on the leaves where the supposed murderer had knelt to cut Jacinto's throat while he was sleeping.

I asked if there were nothing else. Vicente said he had noticed tracks of a big otter.

"Webbed feet?"

Vicente, trying hard to sound more polite than ironical, remarked that it was known otters had webbed feet.

"But, with your permission, did you notice the web?"

Alvar broke in impatiently to say that on leaves, especially where they stuck to whatever touched them, you couldn't tell if the Virgin herself had webbed feet. As for otters, wherever there was new water, they journeyed to look at it. They were bored like the rest of us.

All these excuses were nonsense. They had not examined anything closely, but were not going to admit it. However, they put the identity of the assassin beyond a doubt, and this was the time to tell them what I myself had known for a week past.

"Look, friends! I have seen the animal which made the tracks and I have killed one," I said. "It is, if you like, a sort of big otter. It is also the dwarf. And it crouched by Jacinto while he was sleeping and tore his throat open."

They would not believe it. I may have been too sudden and dramatic. They could neither give me the lie nor laugh at me, which would have ended the conversation; but their general attitude was that I, a mere man of book learning — though, yes, I recognized one end of a horse from the other — could not know more of forest creatures than they who lived in Santa Eulalia. The dwarf could not be an animal, for who ever heard of an animal which could dance or one that drank the blood without eating the flesh?

They trotted out the lot. Live on the other side of the creek. Never go far from the edge of their forest. Do not cross water.

"Well, if all this is so, why would none of you ride alone to the estancia after dark even when there was water in the creek? And why does Joaquín dislike a guitar in Santa Eulalia?"

My obstinacy roused them out of their usual reluctance to talk. It was not true, they said, that none of them would ride alone to the estancia. They were all valiant. It was just that a man on a long ride at night, with no cattle to claim his attention, liked a companion to talk with. It could be there were dwarfs on the other side of the creek, or it could not. But the place was unhealthy. That was known. One had only to observe old Mario who made himself a prisoner every night. As for the guitar, who the devil believed that it could attract dwarfs all the way to Santa Eulalia? Only Joaquin! Good! That did not mean they thought it was true.

"When a priest comes here," Arnoldo explained, "we do not believe all he says. There is much that is very improbable. But he is a man who might speak with the Most Holy Virgin tomorrow or the next day. So a wise man will show some faith. The same with Joaquín."

I replied that I understood all that very well. The beast, however, was so real that it had killed my golden Tesoro before I shot it. I hesitated to say that I had hit it on the nose with a machete.

I now had their instant, warm sympathy. Poor Tesoro! What a loss! Perhaps it had been a jaguar of a strange color. Men had seen such which had more yellow than black in their skins. There was even a story of a white jaguar. Or it could have been a puma, bolder and stronger than usual. They would ride out to see what was left of the carcass and tell me which it was.

"And besides," Alvar pronounced in the true spirit of science, "why look for dwarfs and duendes when we all know that these communists, as they call themselves, killed Jacinto?"

It was no use. Even if they saw the bones of the mustelid, they would swear it was a jaguar with short legs, seeing what they were determined to see and anyway having little knowledge of anatomy beyond that of cattle and horses. If the flooded creek were passable, curiosity might lead one or two of them to the scene; but, as it is, the journey round the marshes, down to the south and back, could not be completed in a day — and, valiant or cautious, not one of them would spend a night in that haunted country.

I had in my saddlebag a couple of bottles of rum for Joaquín and hoped to get some sense out of him before they took effect. He had had to put up with Indian cassava beer for some time and was sure to pass off into the spirit world — a pun which to him would not be one at all — an hour after the corks were pulled.

I told him the story from the time I watched the mustelid at the pool below the ridge up to the death of Tesoro. I told it very slowly with long pauses and invited his comments on the Declaration of Intent. It was difficult to illustrate my meaning by the parallel of the stoat. Small animals in this immensity are ignored, and there is no reliable, intimate natural history. I think it likely that the hunting methods of our *hurón* resemble those of the stoats and weasels, but Indians are only interested in food animals and pets.

Joaquín at least did not doubt the facts. I had seen

the duende and was none the worse. His father, who also saw the duende, had been sick for days.

"So I have always known it was a duende, not a dwarf," he said.

I continued to insist that it was a flesh-and-blood animal, less powerful than the jaguar but ferocious and without respect for man.

"That is the shape which the fear takes."

"But duendes don't die when one blows their brains out, and they don't kill horses."

"If they did not, horses would never die."

We had some more rum while I worked out that fantastic statement. I translate it as meaning that whatever the cause of death — time, worms, the misfortune of breaking a leg — there is always a duende behind it. One cannot prove it isn't so, for we have no machine which will detect the presence or absence of the malevolent duende of ill luck. The virus, that little devil of all devils, was hardly more than a word till the electron microscope revealed its material existence.

This, of course, is afterthought. At the time I was more exasperated than analytical.

"But this duende died," I repeated.

"Why not?"

He whispered in my ear, lest invisible listeners under the thatch should hear him, that he too had killed duendes.

I had another shot at it.

"Friend Joaquín, imagine that a jaguar is tearing

open your belly with its claws! Do you say that your fear is real and the jaguar is not?"

"Man, what foolishness!" — rum was taking over from politeness — "I should feel no more fear."

He may be right. Fear is over, leaving only submission to death.

"Then anything a man is afraid of is a duende?"

"If you came at me with a knife, I should be afraid of you. But you are not a duende."

So there! Logic demands that the moment he fears me I *am* a duende. However, he won't have it. The fact is that he makes no clear distinction between imagined fear and fear of material danger. Thus, when it comes to the mustelid/duende which produces what I call "superstitious" fear, it would take a theologian to define the difference between us.

The power of myth is vaster than I ever imagined. The llaneros will not have it that Jacinto was killed by an animal because they won't admit there could be an animal which they do not know. For Joaquín we are all spirits and the physical shape of the fiend is unimportant. In maintaining that all is illusion he has a better case than the fundamentalist llaneros who are emotionally bound to the old facts and refuse to accept new ones. To fill up the measure of human oddities I can add the Dominican who would at once and sanely accept the mustelids but shuddered at Pedro's corpse.

Now that I am here in silence, except for the patter of the rain and the bird song of Teresa and Chucha in

[230]

the kitchen, I begin to suspect that I too may be making myths for myself. I could be wrong in assuming that it was a fang, not a knife, which ripped open Jacinto's throat. Those fanatics of the National Liberation Army do not shrink from terrorism. They could have found Jacinto sleeping soundly in the ceiba grove and decided that a further lesson would be good for Santa Eulalia. My suggestion that they did not spend the night in the trees but rode straight off over the llano is, after all, mere guesswork.

I must go and see for myself.

[*May 17, Tuesday*]

Today I took Pichón down the east side of the creek. The turbulent yellow river was impassable all the way. I rode Pichón into it at several likely points and we were both very glad to turn tail as soon as he was up to the cinch. Neither man nor beast could have swum across, though it was narrower than it had been at the time of the flood. Acres of mud, smooth and desolate as a sandbank at low tide, stretched along the creek without even the flotsam and jetsam of a beach. There is so little on the llano which can be carried away except dead grass and topsoil.

Where the creek entered the the Guaviare jungle the water had torn down everything in its way, piling up trunks and debris, roaring over and round the obstruction, clearing an avenue through the forest like a troop of bulldozers in line abreast. No accidental bridge or causeway could ever have existed for a minute.

This side of the creek was very different from the dark but open forest to the west through which the mustelids had chased Tesoro. There were only a few outlying trees and groves before one came right up against the green wall. In the shattered woodland the areas of mud showed no tracks but those of birds, proving that the llaneros were right and that the belt between Santa Eulalia and the creek was empty of ground life.

I thought of following the forest edge eastwards to inspect the scene of Jacinto's death, but decided against it. I did not know the country and might spend hours looking for the ceiba grove without any certainty that I had found the right one even if it fitted the description of Alvar and Vicente. I suspect also that my worrying sense of guilt had a subconscious effect. I did not want to know. So I turned for home following the highest mark of the flood.

I had been riding along the tracks for quarter of a mile before I noticed and at once recognized them. All five claws clearly imprinted, which excluded felines. No web, which ruled out otter. There could be no doubt. After I wounded it, the mustelid crossed the creek. My failure to follow up cost Jacinto his life.

I dismounted and tethered Pichón to a stranded tree in a good open position where I could keep him covered if he began to show signs of alarm. Then I explored on foot to see if the spoor — a fine, professional word, that! — could be persuaded to tell any kind of story. My first impression was that the mustelid had come out of the forest to drink. But why take to the open llano when there were plenty of pools and rivulets in cover?

It had followed the edge of the flood plain and three times turned to the water. The level of the creek was now lower, proving that the tracks were made yesterday night or the night before. Twice the animal had chosen spits of land curving out into the torrent, and there was some evidence that it had cautiously paddled. It had then bounded off into the llano where I quickly lost the spoor. Both its gaits, the walk and the high canter, were distinguishable.

Its movements appeared aimless. Repeated drinking was unlikely, so what about a search for carrion brought down by the flood? All the evidence of diet suggested that it touched nothing which was not freshly killed, and only the blood and delicacies of that. Could it have been trying to panic cattle knee-deep in the water? There were no hoof-marks and indeed no sign that cattle had been in this corner for months. The drought had devastated the grazing on this side of the creek as on the other.

I started home, having made no useful deductions at all. We had jogtrotted along in the steaming, sleepy heat when we came to a loop of the creek. On my way down I had cut straight across the base, but I now decided to follow the course of the stream. At the height of the flood the loop had been wiped out, leaving a layer of silt, now dried to powder, which showed indefinite tracks. They were worth following, for the peninsula pointing westwards resembled the configuration of the two spits which the mustelid had visited.

The spoor was there — straight down to the edge of the water and straight back again. I still could not find the answer to what the mustelid was doing out on the open llano when even at night it never moved far from the trees. So it seemed worthwhile to return to the forest and ride slowly along the edge to see if the damp ground in the shade showed anything of interest. This was a productive move. I discovered a clear set of prints where the beast had reentered the trees. It had chosen the same way in that I would myself — a thicket of low, soft growth through which a body could push fairly easily.

Since the mustelid had done what I would do on this occasion, I thought the principle might hold. Suppose I wanted to return to the forest from the creek and did not feel like going back over the desolate mud where there was no hope of bagging even a duck, what would I do? Obviously I would choose a line through high grass which would hide my movements. But there was none. The only cover I could find was a depression about deep enough to keep me off the skyline if I crawled. I rode back to have a look at it. The bottom was boggy, and the prints were there, even the mark of a tail touching the ground. After this triumph of teach-yourself-tracking

I was able to pick up occasional paw marks between depression and peninsula.

The vast clouds which had been towering in the south broke open. Once the lightning had moved away, the downpour was refreshing — a cold shower after a Turkish bath. It allowed my brain to short-cut a little and to appreciate that there were too many tracks. If there had been fewer, I could make a neater story. But nature — to the ignorant — is never neat.

The truth, or part of the truth, seems to be this. After I wounded it, the mustelid crossed the creek, which was then a chain of disconnected pools, and lay up in the Guaviare forest. It started to wander east, possibly attracted by the presence of men and horses. After killing Jacinto and finding no other prey it turned back to the familiar territory of the ridge and the unfailing supply of deer and peccary. But it could not get there. The sudden spate had cut it off from home. Those movements down to the water were exploratory. It was looking for a crossing, a route to the west.

No further evidence turned up on my way home, but I am sure I am right. To predict the mustelid's future movements is nearly impossible, for this is a unique event in the history of this particular animal. Only in this damnable year could it have reached the wrong side of the creek and been caught there.

Since its natural habitat is the deep shade, it must have tried to cross the creek in the forest reaches before ever attempting the open llano. A reasonable guess is

that it made a circuit under the trees, reached the Guaviare wherever the creek enters the river and then
worked up the impassable barrier. There are now two
courses open to it.

One is to raid Santa Eulalia. I hope to God that is not
likely. There is no hunting to lead it in that direction
and it cannot know that at the end of a long, hungry
prowl to the east it would come to horses, and huts with
flimsy fences of cane.

The other is that it will range the llano, hunting a
little further up the creek every night until it reaches
the head of the marshes. There it will find cattle to kill
— will the llaneros put that down to dwarfs? — and
a quick route home to the ridge.

Meanwhile I must observe the strictest precautions
here in the estancia. The animal is in fact a lot more
vulnerable than we are. During the heat of the day it
can only lie up in clumps of palm or cactus. The choice
is very limited. If I cannot detect the right clump, a
horse will. It has little chance in the open and full daylight unless it breaks cover before it is within easy
range. Even then I can run it down, provided Estrellera
is willing to avenge Tesoro. That rather depends on
whether we receive the Declaration of Intent, or turn
the tables and hand it out.

[*May 18, Wednesday*]

Somewhat lighthearted yesterday, weren't you, Ojen? This fellow whom I observe must, in the dubious jargon of psychologists, be a manic-depressive character. Ups and downs. Well, but I seldom have downs. I should say that I am a man who lives on a steady level of mild enjoyment, whose chart would, I admit, show peaks — Chucha, the forest domes, the green flash which follows sunset on the Ilano — but few depressions.

Indecision. That is always the cause. But time is short. This record must be completed. The afternoon is sultry and the sweat pours off me as I write. I would rather be with Chucha, but, if I go through with this, I shall need perfect coordination of eyes, hands and the rifle. Legs, too. Keyed up now. Better stay so.

I set off on Estrellera early this morning. My dear agriculturalists all disapproved of my absence without leave. Mario is hard at it. Well, it won't do any harm to put off the preparation of seedbeds for a day or two until the rains settle down to more regular hours. Back to normal duties, please God, tomorrow!

I was not happy at leaving them. But tilling the soil with rifle in hand like a North American colonist would merely have aroused alarm and agitated questions. In any case everything points to the fact that the mustelids never take to the open in daylight. *Never* is a strong word. A zoologist from Mars observing my normal habits would conclude that I drink and mate freely after

[237]

midnight, but never eat. Exceptions have been known.

I found no more tracks leading to or from the water and cantered off to the few stands of palms on the eastern horizon. Nothing there. Shade was possibly sufficient, but cover was not. I do not know what sweat glands the mustelid possesses or where they are situated; but it is certain that no forest dweller can endure the direct blast of the sun for long.

I was half way to Santa Eulalia when I saw two vultures circling down to the llano more than a mile away to the northeast. I hoped that they were only coming to a cow which had wandered off into the no-man's-land and died or calved there. I could not persuade myself that it was likely. The ground mists of morning were still confusing the lips of the land, and I heard in the silence the squawking and quarreling of the birds long before I could distinguish the clear outline of tall, dead grass, never grazed.

A breeze from the east had got up, so I rode round to give Estrellera the scent of the patch. When she showed no excitement we entered the grass. It was thin, and from my height in the saddle I could see far enough ahead to be fairly safe. I was also fairly confident — nothing is ever more than "fairly" in this amateur pursuit — that the vultures would not have come down unless the mustelid had finished with its kill.

Trailing streaks of excrement they rose heavily, like children's kites with gray and white tails. I approached very cautiously making a circuit round the kill with Estrellera showing strong dislike but no terror. A last vulture took off, and beneath it I got a clear view of red and white. It was long and narrow. I thought the shape was human as I did at the caju tree. When I dismounted and led Estrellera up to it, I saw that it was a mustelid. There was enough left to identify Torn Ear. The ear itself was not in a state to put the matter beyond all doubt, but the right eye was. Since the animal was lying with that side of its head on the ground, the eye had not yet been picked out. A No. 2 shot had pierced it and flattened against the bone of the socket. Damage to mouth and tongue was also cruel. That accounted for the lapping of blood without eating any flesh — if this is not a regular habit. I do not know.

Infinite relief and, of course, pity. I feel it when I shoot to eat. It is odd and illogical that I should feel it even more when I shot to save my life. How can I have more sympathy for a singularly atrocious carnivore than a deer? Does respect come in? Well, this time there will be a clean-picked carcass to be collected at leisure by a cart from Santa Eulalia, if I am here to arrange it.

The track of the beast through the grass was plain enough. I had no difficulty in finding the point where it had entered the patch. Assuming that it would have approached in a straight line — possibly a large assumption for an animal blind on one side and weakened by hunger — I crossed and recrossed the probable trail. I came at last upon tracks in a muddy bottom.

At first they puzzled me. The wounded mustelid seemed to have been progressing by short hops, utterly unlike any of the gaits I knew or any possible gait for an animal of its size. It took me some time to realize that I was looking at the tracks of a pair loping along in single file. They had been made the previous night. I found a dropping which was not yet dry inside.

So back to the patch of cover where the story was completed. I could have worked it out before if Estrellera's movements and the flattening of the grass by vultures had not muddled the evidence. But I had no reason to suspect it was there.

The two beasts left the long grass side by side with a distance of some six feet between them. I was strangely shocked to find clots of blood on the stems which their heads had pushed aside. There could be no doubt that they had chased and killed their wounded relative. Then, with dawn not far off, they set out in hope of cool shade — thank God, not in the direction of Santa Eulalia!

My theory that the sudden, galloping spate of water could have caught mustelids on the wrong side of the creek proved correct; but I never dreamed of active, hungry beasts besides Torn Ear, assuming that the single pair in my immediate neighborhood produced over the years the myth of the dancing dwarfs and that they were the only members of the genus I was ever likely to see.

But even rarities breed, and the larger Mustelidae

such as otter and mink are, I believe, interested and careful parents. The young, like those of the felines, have hunting technique to learn before they are ready to occupy a territory of their own.

The territory of this pair was plainly along the Guaviare between the lower, forested reaches of the creek and the unexplored waterway southwest of the ridge. Pedro confidently expected to find game there. He must have seen open glades, firm ground and game paths while traveling on the Guaviare by canoe.

Why did the pair cross the creek into a forest belt where, according to the llaneros, there was nothing to eat and not a rumor of dwarfs? Failing most unlikely coincidence, I am sure the answer is to be found in the behavior of the half-blinded Torn Ear. Terrified by her first contact with an animal which stood firm and hit back, she bolted across the creek between pools and was followed at a distance by the interested south pair, perhaps stimulated to form pack and hunt in company. Then at some point, due partly to the absence of game and partly to the deadly attraction of a slow and wounded animal, Torn Ear herself became the hunted.

I rode hard for the marshes, giving a cursory glance to the few palms on the way. If this stranded pair had put the growing light behind them and cantered fast for cover, the only place they could find it was by the water, and I did not think they would find much there.

As usual I was not competent to follow the trail over the open llano. However, after a lot of searching I picked up their tracks again on the border of the marshes. There they had separated, one following the edge of the water, the other farther out near the highest flood mark. Both tracks converged on a thicket of tall, brown reeds, canes and a stunted palm or two, where new green shoots were already six inches high.

A lot of this stuff had fallen over in the drought or been battered down by storms. It was waist-high and so tangled that no horse could have penetrated it. A man on foot might have stamped and barged his way through, but he would never have come out alive. The bent reeds formed tents and low lean-to shelters into which the mustelids could slide and from which they could spring without the interruption of any solid growth. The prevailing color was their own. It would have been perfectly possible to step on one without see-ing it.

I dismounted and very nervously smelled the ground where they had entered the reeds. The familiar odor was there, and fresh. Then I rode right round the cover, Estrellera obeying magnificently. I found no tracks lead-ing out again. If they cannot swim, they are there and will be there till dusk.

I must not let them escape and risk another death on my conscience. I am still arguing with myself, but I propose to go out on pretense of taking the evening flight. There will be a good moon in the first quarter. I am confident that I am fast and accurate enough in semidarkness to deal with one, but not two. From the little I have seen of their hunting practice I think it likely that I shall be attacked from behind and from a flank simultaneously. What I want, therefore, is to get them chasing in line. If they will oblige, I can then run in the expected half circle and take refuge in the water where my back will be safe. As I see it, they will stop dead but not retire. Two aimed shots should be enough.

If only I had somebody to tell! Since I have not, I must talk to myself, and this is the best way to do it. When I write, I recognize or think I recognize nonsense; but when I surrender to the incomplete, leaping, pointless conversations of the brain, I am no more capable of precision than any other man.

Here and there in this diary I see signs of a tendency to brood. That is, of course, due to lack of male company and is unimportant. I chose this life and I have been well able to handle it.

Multiple indecision. That's the trouble. It would be easier if I had only to consider the evening ahead of me, to dab a spot of white paint on the foresight and get on with it. But Chucha is interwoven with this business. The other question I must face is: how can I be lonely when I have her? That's the heart of the problem. I love her. I will not be separated from her. I demand that I be married to her.

How would this work out, if I am not about to die? In an intolerable paradox. I am nearly twenty years older than Chucha. But all the arguments which are normally used against such a marriage work the wrong way round. In ten years' time or a bit more she will be no longer this firefly, charged with light during the day, regiving it after sunset. She will be a wrinkled, ignorant Indian like Teresa, and I a successful scientist — in the world's sense — at the peak of my career and the prime of life.

What do you say to that, Don Ojen? I say that I do not care. Suppose I had a daughter disfigured in body and stunted in mind by disease, would I stop loving her? But she is not my daughter — she is a pet from the forest. Very well, Indians cherish a pet till it dies. There is no way out.

What vile, selfish arguments in a void! How cynical can I get? Let us imagine that Don Ojen has killed his dragons. In the eyes of whatever blasted society he frequents, he would be a person of interest who could get away with whatever he pleased. His eccentricity and his little Indian wife would be all in character. The bastard could go around wearing silver spurs and a comic hat. For God's sake, what nonsense!

It is Chucha herself I must think of. That little golden organism is compounded of love and nothing else. It is made to love and be loved. Am I to be "sensible" and hand it over to a Joaquín or an Alvar, or set it up in a Bogotá flat for Valera and his friends?

I will not do it. A vile betrayal! Yet even if I were to spend my life in one of the Andean capitals she would be lost. So imagine her in London, with nothing she understood, nothing that gave her happiness or ever could, her life me and nothing else.

Now, on a step further! My duty to Santa Eulalia, to Mario and Teresa. I have to go out tonight. Am I afraid? Yes. Am I unwilling? No. Why? Because you refuse to face your responsibilities, Don bloody Ojen. That is not true. What is true is that I refuse to imagine life with her or without her. I therefore offer Death a chance. I say to Death: settle it for me, but, by God, I'll fight you all the way!

Hysterical! High-sounding nonsense! I must try to picture Valera trying to suppress a smile. But one thing is certain. Valera wouldn't leave duendes around on the wrong side of the creek. Valera wouldn't muddle his obvious duty with a lot of fifth-rate drivel on whether or not Chucha could make a London hostess. What it all boils down to is that I am prepared to be a little more rash than I would otherwise be. And let us leave the precise meaning of that "otherwise" to psychologists who have nothing better to do.

[10:30 P.M.]

That is over, if it is. I cannot eat. I must be alone a little. Chucha, I know, is frightened. Those round, so gentle eyes stared at me, only understanding that there was no crossing the water to so foreign an island. Women — even this firefly — seem able to forget

[245]

weeks of truth and to read a false significance into two minutes. Perhaps she feels rejected. But I must have time to relax. Let me finish this record, this diary which has become a damned duty to zoology, and I shall be with her again. Nothing but entirety of spirit will comfort her.

I left half an hour before sunset. I carried the rifle in front of me so that she could not distinguish it from the gun. I know very well that she always runs to the wall and looks over it after me. And a lot of use that wall is now after the rains!

It was a clear evening with little chance of rain in the early part of the night. I walked fast up the marshes and checked the tracks before the sun went down. The mustelids were still in the reeds. As the last of the duck were splashing on to the water I moved off some three hundred yards into the open. The wind, such as it was, blew from the llano allowing them to pick up my scent. They were not likely to ignore me. They had eaten very little of their relative, probably finding all but the blood distasteful.

Visibility in the last of the dusk, with a moon in the first quarter, was good. Sure killing range was about thirty yards, but so was charging range. When they started to close in, I hoped they would dance for me to get a better look. If I then missed, as I well might — the target being as narrow as a man — the chase was on.

In the singing silence I thought I heard the canes

cracking and shifting. Before I could be sure a last skein of geese came over and swam around with soft, sleepy chatterings. For half an hour I had to endure a soundless, dubiously empty half circle of silvered peace, continually looking behind me to ensure that the other half was empty.

Half an hour was too much and all wrong. I had believed that the action would begin as soon as they had extricated themselves from the binding, difficult cover along the marshes. It was certain that after sunset hunger and habit would compel them to leave it.

I detected a faint whiff of musk on the wind, so I turned my back on the cover and kept the main watch in the opposite direction. I had expected that one would attack straight up from the water while the other worked round a flank; so long as I knew which flank, I could then run and bring them clearly into sight on my trail. But attack from the llano puzzled me. Although it was more in accordance with their downwind hunting, it seemed to me that they ran a risk of driving their game into the water and safety. I decided that they knew best, that experience must have taught them how to turn me towards the llano.

I write: "I decided." But my racing guesswork merely kept half a jump ahead of what their instinctive movements ought to be and decided very little. The only available fact was that one of them, in spite of a natural impatience, had spent a long time working into position out on the open llano. It stood to reason that the other must be on the edge of the dead canes in order to signal me away from the water.

It was therefore essential to pinpoint the fellow waiting on the marshes. I tried to do this by lying down so as to get a bright background of water through the gaps in the rushes. But the scent of musk had become a little stronger, showing that the other was beginning to close. I was unpleasantly aware that the back of my neck was exposed and that I could not turn round quickly. So I got up and walked slowly towards the cover.

The mustelid's curiosity, its tendency to inspect before committing itself, gave it away. The outline was as vague as a tree stump but bobbed up and down against the stars. I took the outside chance — more to relieve my nerves than with any assurance of killing — lay down, took my time and fired. It paid no attention. The foolhardy courage of the stoat or just utter ignorance of man and his resources? I had ample opportunity for a second shot which either scored an outer in the thick skin or was close enough to convince the mustelid that its prey was being impertinent. The dancing stopped, and I caught a glimpse of it creeping unhurriedly, belly to ground, straight at me before I lost sight of it among the outlying clumps of rushes. This was out of its normal hunting pattern. I had become an enemy, like the jaguar, to be intimidated.

My own pattern was also disturbed. I did not see how I could now line the pair up and bring them after me to the edge of the water. One was in front, meaning business, and the other was somewhere out in the llano waiting for the next move of the quarry. I lay down again so that my silhouette could not be seen against the moonlit sky. I was upwind of the fellow I had annoyed, and there was a good chance of my spotting him before he spotted me.

While I was wishing to God that I had never fired those two shots and muddled the natural course of the hunt, a long strip of black cloud, which I had been too busy to notice, drifted over the moon. Starlight would have been good enough for close quarters if my eyes had become accustomed to it, but this sudden blotting out of a silver world blinded me. It looked as if I might need the machete again. I had not got it. I was stripped for running.

Nothing happened. No sound. No scent. Loss of contact. My reading of the position then was that I hadn't a hope. My reading now is that the mustelid's night sight, like my own, needed a moment to adjust itself; meanwhile, the compulsion to avenge annoyance faded away and was replaced by the instinct to continue the hunt. It must have changed direction and passed across my right flank to join up with the other.

It was at this point that I probably received the Declaration of Intent, but there was quite enough general panic to be resisted without attending to details of clinical analysis. I prefer to put it this way: the involuntary compulsion to run coincided with my deliberate plan to run. So I ran. All very pretty, but one essential fact was missing. I did not know what lead I had.

I think I would have bolted straight for the water if there had been any quick way of reaching it through the thick stuff where the mustelids had spent the day. As it was, I was forced to stick to my original intention and run more or less parallel to the marsh. When at last I dared to turn my head, I could see nothing; but instinct insisted that they were committed and on my trail.

The moon cleared for a moment and I looked behind again. There they were, both in line and producing the leaping-porpoise effect exactly as when hunting the peccary. The target was impossibly narrow and oscillating as I had foreseen. One, perhaps. Two, no.

I began the curve — the wrong way from their point of view. The distance between us and the distance to the blessedly gleaming water were about the same. A man sprinting could hold them over a hundred yards. Horse or deer could leave them standing, if it used its speed and kept straight. But even Tesoro was run down. They do not have the decent doubt of the felines. They know what the end will be.

I charged through the rushes and into the water, went over my knees in mud, stuck fast and could only turn to fire very clumsily. The leader was sitting up and slavering at me. I shot it through the body but missed any immediately vital spot. Water or no, it then sprang at me. I finished it with a heart shot almost on the

[250]

muzzle of the rifle, throwing myself sideways to avoid the falling body.

When I struggled up again, the other had gone. The dead mustelid was floating out of reach in a fan of red water. It had taken up the position of a sinking ship, buttocks and tail above the surface. If that does represent the relative buoyancy of the animal in life, it would certainly find swimming laborious. There will not be much of it left to collect. Alligators should now be working upstream, and what the eels cannot manage they will finish.

I pulled myself out by the reed stems and scraped the mud from my watch. Incredibly, from first contact to finish, only fifty-five minutes. I thought of it then as finish, for the disruption of the hunting pattern was complete, and the lesson surely enough for any animal. In my relief I overlooked the vital stimulus of hunger. This particular individual, whose normal range was far away to the southwest, had no experience of an upright beast of familiar outline which ran, but made a loud noise and was associated with the dangers of water. Its vague picture of an urgent present, lacking cause and effect, only inhibited action without forbidding it.

In any case half of me was ready to welcome a second meeting if the mustelid did not continue its course to the north and the head of the marshes. Now that I had got my breath back and the foresight had stopped wobbling, the odds were acceptable. Conditions were as good as could be expected, though the angle of the moonlight was treacherous, and folds of ground, hardly perceptible in daylight, were in black shadow.

My right flank was protected by the water, my left a target area where nothing within thirty yards could live if I were fast enough. There was of course no protection against attack from behind, but by glancing round after I had passed clear of any possible line of approach I more or less secured myself against surprise. After I had walked a cautious half mile or more I began to curse my sight. The outline of the black dips was fuzzier than it should have been. The stars had lost their brilliance. The change was so slight and gradual that I really thought it was the result of intense straining of the eyes. Not until the crescent of the moon was also hazed did I realize that a ground mist was thickening.

In another few minutes I was in almost complete darkness, and the moon only a lighter patch of sky. I could just make out the water and keep direction; otherwise visibility was down to nothing. I stopped to think. Not that it did any good. My position was desperate if the mustelid had not lost interest. I tried my pocket flashlight, but it was worse than useless. The far end of the beam showed a mere, blurred oval of llano, leaving me with even less night sight than I had.

There was no scent to help. In fact all my senses were out of action except hearing. I would have been thankful to receive the "superstitious" fear, which at least would have told me for certain what I was in for and perhaps turned the rifle in the right direction. But even that was absent. I was empty of fear and could understand what Joaquín meant when he said that fear was over as soon as the prey went down under the teeth and claws.

Always there were little noises from the marsh: the splash of fish or frog, the rustle of reeds as they parted to let through the invisible. Under the pall of the mist the faint activity of my unseen companions was hushed but continuous. Without interruption of the business of living they let my footsteps pass. I could imagine that they were friendly or that I was no longer of any importance.

Ten paces behind me two duck rose with a whir and a clatter. I jumped round and fell on one knee, instinctively meaning to bring the muzzle of the rifle under the body as it rose for the final spring. The mustelid, too, was startled by the duck, I heard a squelch as it slipped on the edge of the mud and then the unmistakable, soft sound of a leap to firmer ground.

It could kill me when it pleased. Walking backwards was no use. One fall and it had me. Standing still in the hope of that last split-second shot was no use either. I tried it. My follower also stopped still. After we had covered a few hundred yards I began to learn exactly where it was. My ears could pick up the footfalls, some real, some no doubt imaginary. There were times when I knew the beast was far behind, times when it was so close that I would swing round and cover nothing. I dared not fire. I might wound. That would infallibly

[253]

end this state of neutrality. My only chance of safety seemed to lie in letting it follow me like a dog at heel for as long as it would.

I strode out more boldly, for there was nothing else I could do. I remember and repeat that I was emptied of fear — so much so that I controlled myself by analyzing the validity of my repugnance at what was coming to me. To be eaten — why such horror of it? Death in war, death in our suicidal transport, we accept both; or, if we refuse to accept, at least they are not nightmares. Yet this death, quick, clean, a last offering of hospitality to a fellow hunter, men think the most terrible.

The water tempted me, but I should be floundering in mud before I was out of reach. So we walked on, never hurrying lest one or the other should end this intimacy. When I felt that it was too close and that hunger was overcoming caution, I would turn round gently. Then there was silence. I could never be sure that I had seen it. I think I never did. It can flatten itself to less than the thickness of a man. Even in full daylight one cannot be certain, as I had already discovered, where is the bone and where is skin. The weasel — tiny, but of similar anatomy — can both kill a rabbit and pass through a wedding ring. That should be remembered by the millionaire who thinks he can shoot fast or the proud Brazilian hunter who is not afraid to use a spear as his second line of defense.

We walked in our curious companionship of death until I received a waft of musk. It was not for me; it was for the horses. Much later than the mustelid I picked up the smell of the corral spreading under the mist. That was the first sign that I was nearing home; till then I could not have said whether I had two more miles to go or was already near the outlet of the creek. I knew at once that the beast had broken contact and that I could at last run with safety. It was very necessary. In spite of all the rules, there could be a little gossiping by an open window.

I took the chance that the mustelid was over on the far side investigating the corral, and came in over the rubble of the east wall. Chucha heard me and flung open the kitchen door, staying in the light to welcome me. I shouted to her to shut it, which she did not, and rushed across the courtyard nearly knocking her over in my anxiety.

The three of them drew away and stared at me, for I was plastered with black mud on hair, face and clothes. I must have made a convincing duende straight out of the depths of the marsh. That may have contributed to my escape. Even to the efficient night sight of my follower I was black against black, never clearly distinguishable, smelling of foul water.

Chucha asked me where the duck were. The fire and the spit had long been ready. After all, I never failed. I ignored her. I could not help it. I had no speech. She may have thought that I suspected she was making fun of me. I went straight to the laboratory and the whisky bottle. My clothes slopped off me onto the floor. When I had put on a dressing gown so as not to shock her blasted peasant prudery, I called to Teresa to take the mess away and rinse it. The woman stammered that the moon was clear again and that she would go out at once and fetch water from the well.

They are all mad, when there is nothing but a closed door between them and death. Just because Mario and Teresa know or think they know that the pitiable dwarfs are as solid as themselves, they are free of anxiety. What curiosities they are! Or perhaps we are all alike. Warn a man that the devil will get him if he doesn't do what he is told, and he obeys trembling. Warn him that his life is in danger, and the effect will wear off in a week.

I made no mistake with Teresa. I told her that there was a duende in the night and that I had seen it. Drastic, for what I say is the word of God. If now there were an accident without obvious cause, I can imagine them seized by such a concentration of twelve years' suppressed terror that they would rather fly hand in hand into the empty llano than stay another moment in the estancia. But it doesn't matter. When they see the dead animal tomorrow and I explain the source of the rumors which have oppressed them ever since the disappearance of Cisneros. I can trust their sound common sense.

The dead animal. Yes. It will not go far from the only food and at first light it will take to the shade of Mario's old house or one of the ruined, overgrown cabins. For such close quarters I shall use the 16-bore — quick, certain, and blast more effective than a single bullet at what is going to be the range.

Chucha came in some ten minutes ago while I was deep in this record. She had the impertinence to ask me why I had frightened the pair just because I had fallen in and bagged no duck. Impertinence? Or a daughter's utter trust in my gentleness? I told her to leave me alone, to go to bed and I would come. She saw that I was shaking with nerves and whisky. Not very tactful after her experience in a dim past. But I have to unwind, God damn it!

Women's lack of steady confidence is so absurd. She looked at me and seemed to wither as if love had suddenly come to an end. What does she think I am up to? Disillusioned with her and looking for another wife among the dwarfs? Well, of course she cannot know more than I tell her. If it were daylight I should find the child had run outside to talk to her sapling. I lack imagi